RESOURCES BY KEN DAVIS

How to Live with Your Parents Without Losing Your Mind
I Don't Remember Dropping the Skunk, But I Do Remember Trying to Breat
Fire Up Your Life
Jumper Fables
How to Speak to Youth . . . and Keep Them Awake at the Same Time
Lighten Up!
Lighten Up! audio
Sheep Tales
How to Live with Your Kids When You've Already Lost Your Mind
Secrets of Dynamic Communication

Find all of Ken's comedy videos, audios, and other resources
at www.kendavis.com or Ken Davis Productions,
P.O. Box 745940, Arvada, CO 80006-5940; (303) 425-1319.

A FAMILY DEVOTIONAL READER

Sheep Tales

THE BIBLE ACCORDING TO
THE ANIMALS WHO WERE THERE

Ken Davis

ZondervanPublishingHouse

Grand Rapids, Michigan

A Division of HarperCollinsPublishers

We want to hear from you. Please send your comments about this book to us in care of the address below. Thank you.

ZondervanPublishingHouse
Grand Rapids, Michigan 49530
http://www.zondervan.com

Sheep Tales
Copyright © 2001 by Ken Davis

Requests for information should be addressed to:

ZondervanPublishingHouse
Grand Rapids, Michigan 49530

Library of Congress Cataloging-in-Publication Data
Davis, Ken.
    Sheep Tales : the Bible according to the animals who were there / Ken Davis.
      p.   cm.
    Includes bibliographical references.
    ISBN 0-310-22758-5 (hardcover)
    1. Animals in the Bible—Fiction. 2. Bible—History of Biblical events—Fiction.
I. Title
PS3554.A93494 S54 2001
813'.54—dc 21
                                                     00-051261

This edition is printed on acid-free paper.

Published in association with Wolgemuth and Associates, Inc.

Illustrations by Gareth Andrews
Interior design by Todd Sprague

Printed in the United States of America

02 03 04 05 06 /❖ DC/ 10 9 8 7 6 5 4 3

• •

This book is lovingly dedicated to my granddaughter
Kailee Brielle Scheer
In the prayerful hope that God will steal her heart
as completely as she stole mine.

Contents

Acknowledgments

I want to thank Rob Suggs for his editorial contribution to this book and Drew Blankman for keeping a close eye on my words to be sure my stories stayed consistent with scriptural truth.

A special thank-you to Gareth Andrews, who went way above the call of duty to contribute his talent to this book. His artwork is well-known to a small world. I am so grateful he has allowed me to share it with you.

Finally I thank Robert Wolgemuth, Danny deArmas, and Dan Marlow, who believed in this book, fought for its publication, and encouraged me every step of the way. Without their efforts the Sheep Tales might never have been told.

Introduction

For me, it all goes back to the pictures—wonderful pictures that decorate my earliest memories. All I need to do is close my eyes to see, once again, all those colorful scenes and set pieces from my Sunday school Bible. What child wouldn't respond to them? I can see daring Daniel kneeling in the lions' den; agonized Abraham lifting his knife, prepared to surrender his son to God; and, of course, majestic Moses standing before the great parting tides of the sea.

Early in my life, the great stories of the Bible captivated my imagination. They're filled with unforgettable images, culminating in the focal scene that towers above them all. It's the image painted on canvas more than any other, depicted in more sermons and engraved more deeply in our minds than any human event—the image of a man hanging on a cross. And even so, that image gives way to one final, ultimate picture: the image of a deserted tomb and a discarded shroud.

These are scenes potent enough to bring heartfelt tears in any theater of the world, in any language or setting, and in places where the name of Jesus has yet to be spoken.

Yet for a significant portion of my life, the story of the cross of Christ never brought those tears from me. Somehow the basic emotions of the story failed to resonate in my heart, and I wondered why I couldn't feel the things I knew I ought to be feeling. What was wrong with me?

Then one day a uniquely anointed author came along to help me finally make the emotional connection I craved so deeply. This author understood the dusty, stained-glass barriers to finding fresh emotions for a too-familiar story. He set out to write the tale in a new way that would catch me off guard and "steal past those watchful dragons" (as this author put it)—the dragons denying me the rich tears I needed to shed.

This author told me the story from another perspective. For the first time, the truth and power of the crucifixion snapped into painful, poignant focus.

The author was C. S. Lewis, and he brought forth water from the stone of my heart with his wonderful series of books titled *The Chronicles of Narnia*. Aslan the lion held court there, standing as the potent symbol of the loving and powerful Christ. There was nothing dusty or stained-glass about *that* lion. When I read the account of the sacrificial giving of his life on the stone altar, I wept aloud—not for Aslan the lion, but for the Christ of the cross. Yes, this was how I had felt all along, deep within. C. S. Lewis set my emotions free.

Lewis found a secret door that helped me sneak past those watchful dragons of familiarity. The story of Aslan did not substitute for the biblical account; it illuminated it in a piercing new light, from a different angle than the one the painters and sculptors and Sunday school teachers had been able to show me. It drove me back to the Scriptures with fresh passion, to see and feel and embrace all that I had missed before.

And that's why I've brought these tales to you. I came to perceive the truth about the fragile relationship between fact and feeling. Emotion alone is deceitful and misleading. Truth alone is cold and tedious. But emotion driven by truth is something else entirely. It endows truth with a heartbeat. It brings biblical truths to the door of our hearts, where we might embrace them and welcome them to settle in and take residence. That's the prayer I have for this book.

Sheep Tales was written with the hope that it would be read by people of all ages. Be on the lookout for familiar characters in these pages: You and your friends lurk here! Be willing to encounter attitudes and actions you may recognize with a twinge of discomfort. Be prepared to identify with the struggles and the triumphs as your very own.

Little ones will easily grasp the lessons here—especially if they are fortunate enough to have these stories read to them by a loving and caring adult with a comfortable lap. As the author, my greatest desire is that this book would be read with the entire family present.

I urge you to read the original biblical accounts that inspired each of these tales. Even if you're familiar with the great narratives of the Bible, go back and take one more look. These stories will never fail to greet you with a fresh, new message.

I hope you will let these whimsical stories capture your imagination and touch you with laughter—and maybe a few tears. But most of all, I hope you'll be transported from appealing fantasy to compelling reality. I hope you'll find a new door, or perhaps just a small window, for stealing in to take a great look at the volume Galya, our teller of *Sheep Tales,* calls "the Great Book."

And when you've closed its cover again, I hope you will have found a treasure there—the signpost that points to deep joys that *Sheep Tales* can only hint at. These are the joys of finding and knowing the One who guards the flock through the night, the Good Shepherd who loves and tends sheep of every age, color, and variety—even stray sheep like you and me.

1 Galya and Edgar

GALYA

Galya was dreaming—and it was a good one!

In Galya's dream, he skipped across a beautiful green meadow teeming with lush grass waving in the wind. The sky was blue and the air was cool. The meadow and its delicious food seemed to stretch as far as the eye could see. Galya wandered past wolves in this dream, and the wolves merely offered a smile. He watched with wide eyes as two small lambs snuggled deep into the furry mane of a lion for a nap.

What a place! In this meadow there were no predators. A wild and wonderful feeling of freedom washed over him as he leaped across the fields and played without fear. Of course it was a dream, he knew that—but who cared? Perhaps he would never awaken.

Of course, he did.

A sound invaded Galya's dream—an unpleasant sound that had no place at all in such a wonderful world. It was the sound of a hollow growl. And Galya was suddenly and abruptly awake.

In the waking world, a gate was swinging open. Galya's eyes burned as yellow light danced through the darkened sheep pen. There was no way he could comprehend that the gentle slumber and the delightful dream, just snatched from his grasp, were gone, never to return. He couldn't know that the following moments would change his life forever. He struggled to his feet as the muffled sounds clearly became the familiar, droning voices of the men. He blinked away the sleep as the flickering light revealed the image of two of them, searching the pen with a lamp.

Galya's racing heart began to settle back into a normal cadence. Perhaps he could go back to sleep and rejoin the wonderful dream. He knew there was no need to assume the worst—shepherds often checked their sheep at night. Occasionally the men would remove a lamb for a thing they called *sacrifice*. And sacrifice was something Galya had given a lot of thought to. It was a mysterious thing, something the other sheep revered and feared at the same time. Galya had been taught that to be chosen for sacrifice was an honor. It seemed to be a proud thing. But it was also clear to him that those who were chosen never returned. It was hard for him to conceive of any proud thing being worthy of death, especially his own death.

Galya was young, after all. He had his whole life before him— all the abundant adventures and opportunities that sheep life offered. There were romances to be explored, games to be played, escapades to be pursued.

That's why Galya had certain fears about being selected for sacrifice, no matter how great an honor it was presumed to be. He supposed the thing would come without warning. Couldn't it happen at any time, on any day, while he grazed happily or napped peacefully? And then there was the undeniable truth that he was the perfect candidate for sacrifice. He had such fine wool. He was admired by all the ewes and rams, and some of them even looked to him as a leader. Galya knew he was special—and the men were always looking for sheep who were special.

But Galya had one thing in his favor: He was pretty crafty for a sheep. He had watched closely, and he knew what kinds of things the men checked for—perfect skin, wool that held no spots or blemishes. He had worked out a plan to remove himself from consideration.

Galya kept an eye on the dwellings where the men stayed. And every time one of the men would come to select a sheep and lead it away, Galya would roll in the mud. His coat would be filthy; his smell would be uninviting, to say the least. Whenever the men drew near, Galya would walk with a limp and make pitiful little bleating sounds.

He knew what he wanted, but much more than that, he knew what he *didn't* want. He didn't want to be taken away for some ritual he did not understand—some ritual no sheep ever returned from. And so far his plan was working and his life had been spared.

Galya thought about all these things as he shook away the sleep. It would be so much nicer to be thinking about that beautiful dream, the one with the friendly wolves and lions and the acres of delicious grass. But the dreamy details were fading quickly now as the men made their rounds. The shepherds moved slowly, flooding each little corner with light, rubbing their hairy chins and speaking in soft tones. Galya's heartbeat had almost returned to normal as the men moved toward him and raised their lamps so that he blinked away the glare.

There was nothing to worry about; they always passed him by for some older, finer specimen of sheep. Tonight Galya was relieved to realize he was far from a fine specimen. His wool was matted with hay and dirt from the pen. Drool was on his chin. His eyes blinked sleepily as he waited for the men to move to the next candidate. In another moment he would be snoozing again. But the next moment didn't follow the usual pattern.

As Galya began to lay his head back down, a rope slid suddenly and tightly under his chin and around his neck. Hands were gripping his ears and his legs. Then there was a harsh pull as they yanked him to his feet, and he skidded across the hay toward the gate. Galya was in the moonlight, between the men, and they were leading him away.

His heart tried to take in the truth of it. His mind tried to catch up and think ahead. But he was not prepared for this thing that had struck like a thunderbolt. In his confusion he made out the words from the men's lips, the words they always said when a sheep had been chosen for sacrifice: "God will be pleased."

Galya didn't know how much time had passed before he heard another gate creak open, and he found himself in a new pen—one he had never seen before. He was left there alone, but he had no intention of staying. As soon as the men were out of sight, he searched every inch of the pen for a weak spot, some thin section in the hedge he could apply his nose to and force an opening. Maybe he could escape.

But there was no weak spot. He began to feel more desperate, and at least a dozen times he hurled his body into the sides of the pen, only to fall back, bruised and weak. Finally he just lay where he had fallen, too tired to stumble to his feet another time. What was the use? He lay panting until finally, in sheer exhaustion, he fell into a fitful sleep and tried desperately to recall the beautiful dream—the world completely free of angry wolves and shepherds who led sheep to their deaths. But that dream had slid from his grasp, only to be replaced by nightmares that seemed destined to come true.

Galya had no way to know how long he slept. But it was clear that the sun had risen above the horizon and was nudging the cool air from the misty morning. Even with his eyes clamped shut, the soft rays of the sun pushed a radiant red light through his eyelids. The light flickered momentarily as a shadow swept by. Galya heard the whisper of wings.

"Edgar," he murmured. The last thing he needed now was a visit from Edgar. Edgar was drawn to trouble as flies are drawn to a carcass.

Galya knew that Edgar had landed nearby and was taking in the scene through his cloudy, half-blind eyes. Edgar would be gazing hard into the pen, listening, testing the air to be certain it was truly his old friend, Galya. It had to be Edgar. Galya buried his head deeper in the dirt and waited for the crusty cackle.

EDGAR

It came, all right—a crusty cackle. "And where is your God now, Little Lamb?"

"My *name* is *Galya*," Galya snapped.

Edgar was a friend, in a way, but he was the kind of friend who requires plenty of patience. He was that kind of friend whom, if you weren't careful, you might confuse with an enemy. He pushed friendship to its limits.

He mocked and challenged whatever Galya said, always looking for an argument. Edgar called Galya "Little Lamb" simply to embarrass him. He had sat quietly on a branch and heard Galya's mother calling him "God's little lamb," even though he was a grown sheep. Edgar took advantage of little details like that.

Edgar was not the kind of friend to offer encouragement or comfort. He was like a bad itch under Galya's skin. Galya wasn't quite sure why he put up with Edgar in the first place, and he certainly couldn't figure out why Edgar stayed around when all he ever did was badger and bother him.

As a baby raven, Edgar had clung to his mother much longer than his siblings had; he had simply had no choice. All the birds knew about his eyes—the eyes that had never worked properly. Edgar didn't have the razor-sharp vision that is the pride of every raven. He could make out a bit of light; he could detect motion. But it was a vague and misty world that passed before Edgar's eyes. His view of the world was like peering through milky ice.

Because of his problem, Edgar's mother had prudently taught him to be careful at all times. Nothing could be taken for granted. On his own, Edgar knew he had to be tough and he had to be quick. So Edgar peered intently through his half-blind eyes. He attacked first and asked questions later. What seemed like some tempting

His mother often told him that his heart was so big she wondered how it fit in his body. She taught him to give thanks for the blessings of each day.

morsel moving across the ground, usually turned out to be nothing more than a leaf or a bit of weed blowing in the wind.

Still, every once in awhile, Edgar would be rewarded with real food—the kind the strong-sighted birds could get. His first success had been a juicy beetle, a triumph he would never forget. Once he had even caught a mouse, a treat usually reserved for high-flying hawks or stealthy owls.

He lived for these rare rewards, and he strained his eyes and listened carefully. But his finest gift was his nose. A raven's main diet comes from the bodies of fallen, lifeless animals, and early in life Edgar developed a keen ability to smell dead things. It's true that most ravens don't smell so well, for they can hover high and use their fine eyesight to find the food they need.

But Edgar didn't have such eyes, and he had developed his sense of smell until he could detect a fallen rabbit or chipmunk from a mile away. His mother had taught him how to fly. Oh, the other ravens could fly circles around Edgar, but even with his limited eyesight he could stay aloft and hunt with his nose. Edgar refined an ingenious method for zeroing in on the exact location of a carcass. He glided in wide, low circles, testing the air for the unmistakable smell of death.

He sniffed—and he listened. When ravens gather for a feast, the chatter is high-pitched and intense. Some birds tear off their portions, swoop to a nearby branch, and sit there chuckling and chortling as they enjoy their dinner. Others circle high above, shouting in hungry anticipation. On a still day, their raspy exclamations can be heard for miles. Some sing for joy, some cackle in greed, and some exult in praise.

But not Edgar. It had been a long time since anything resembling praise emerged from his throat.

His mother often told him that his heart was so big she wondered how it fit in his body. She taught him to give thanks for the blessings of each day. She told him that a powerful and loving Bird-Maker, one who knew and loved every feather on his body, had been the one who carefully put him together, beak by feather by claw. His name was *God*.

What beautiful words his mother had! Edgar had loved to hear stories of God, the Bird-Maker, who had made not only the beautiful birds but a wide and wonderful world of amazing animals and simple seedlings and delicate autumn leaves. How he wished that someday, by some marvelous magic, it would be possible for him to see these wonders with his own eyes.

He hoped and dreamed, and he kept a smile in his heart. But his dreams were shattered on a crisp fall morning, the day his heart closed up for good.

Edgar had continued to return to the nest long after his brothers and sisters had gone to live on their own. He needed the help and protection he could find there. One morning he awoke and stretched, but he didn't hear his mother's soft call from a nearby branch. Every morning she would call and he would answer. Then he would follow her in flight as they searched for what his mother called "the provision of God." But this morning he didn't hear her voice, and he couldn't see her familiar blurry form.

Edgar cried out several times, softly at first and then with all his might. He turned his head from side to side, searching in vain for some tiny movement, for the shadow that would announce her arrival. How he wished he could see. He continued to call until midday. He was not afraid to fly without her; he had done it many times. If he watched carefully for the big landmarks she'd taught him to recognize, he could find his way back to the nest. The reason he didn't fly away now was that his mother might return, find him gone, and become concerned. Edgar could not bear the thought of causing her one moment of worry.

As late afternoon moved toward evening, Edgar was still calling out. But his voice had become strained and his throat swollen. His desperate calls had become rasps. Then he heard it—the unmistakable voice of a raven overhead, screeching with excitement because food had been spotted.

This was good news for Edgar. He was tired and worried, but he was also very hungry; he hadn't had a bite to eat all day. The voice of the calling raven was easy to recognize; it was Iago, one of the boldest and strongest scavengers in the area. And now Iago had found a meal for them all—which meant that other ravens would hear his announcement and come from miles around. One of them would surely be his mother, and she would greet him joyfully and help him get his fair share of the food. Edgar's heart raced in anticipation.

Then the wind shifted, and Edgar smelled it. The aroma was a strong one, so he knew the meal must be close to the nest. He knew from his earliest training that if he waited, he may have to share his meal with dozens of ravens or, worse yet, he may end up with nothing at all. Edgar stepped gingerly to the edge of the nest, made a little hop, and glided toward the feast. He was the first to arrive, and he was delighted that, at least for a few moments, he could dine in peace. Three more hops brought him to the blurry form of the fallen creature. Then a familiar aroma washed over him. He reeled with horror and stumbled backward. The fallen, lifeless thing on the ground—it was his mother.

Edgar was paralyzed. He could not fly away; he couldn't even move. He could only stand with his wings braced clumsily against the ground, trembling over the cold and unmoving body of feathers he

had known as his mother. A shriek of grief and agony spilled from his throat, and he began to weep harder and more helplessly than he had ever known it was possible to weep.

Though Edgar was scarcely aware of anything else, a shadow flitted by in a whisper. It was the form of a raven—the one named Iago.

The newly arrived raven stood cautiously and curiously at first, peering quickly back and forth between Edgar and the fallen body of his mother. Then, with a squawk, he hopped sideways toward the tiny carcass. He bent forward to eat.

Edgar cried out in rage and attacked, his claws and beak ripping at the air. With a mocking chuckle, Iago easily sidestepped Edgar's desperate lunge. He started toward the carcass. Edgar pulled himself upright and whirled toward Iago, who was again poised over his mother. At this one awful moment of his life, Edgar was grateful he could not see fine and focused details.

Before he could charge again, a screech of excitement burst the air. Another raven had arrived on the scene—and then another and another. Within a moment, there were hungry ravens—too many to count. His mother disappeared behind a blur of black, bustling forms. Edgar didn't care how many there were; he had to stop them.

The other ravens avoided his wild, leaping attacks fairly easily and went about their gruesome business. They would step deftly aside or hop into the air as Edgar rushed past, and then they would return to their meal. Edgar kept fighting, kept leaping, kept sobbing. The half-blind raven fought until he had expended every last ounce of strength.

Finally the grief-stricken bird gathered himself and staggered through the night air to his nest. He burrowed as deep as he could into the soft but lonely interior, trying not to hear the terrible, laughing commotion of the feast below. The warm and pleasant smell of his mother permeated the feathers that lined the nest. But that aroma, once so comforting and secure, now tore a great, gaping wound in Edgar's heart. He finally fell asleep, exhausted and confused, and as he slept, a strange thing happened within him. The wound in his heart closed up. It did not heal, mind you; a thick, new skin grew over it. All the softness in Edgar was replaced by roughness. The smile in his heart distorted itself into an ugly sneer.

The only one he had ever loved was gone, and there was nothing left but hatred and mistrust and anger. *The Creator? The Bird-Maker?* A likely story. Why hadn't *He* shown up to save his mother? As for the patient hope of someday seeing the wondrous world with fresh eyes, that was gone as well. Who cared to see such an ugly world as this one?

The wound, of course, had not healed under that new skin. No one could see it, but it remained as an ache within Edgar every lonely day of his life. All Edgar could do was inflict his aching, hurtful misery on others, and that's exactly what he did. And even now, perched on one of the branches that formed the walls of Galya's pen, he had nothing but misery to share with one of the only animals willing to be his friend—a sheep who was facing certain slaughter.

"I searched for you in the common pen," said Edgar to Galya. "They told me you had been taken here."

Edgar waited patiently for a response, but the sheep remained motionless and silent. "Now you will pay the ultimate price to the God you adored." Again there was no response. Edgar cocked his head and hopped closer. "Of course, if He were as wonderful as you say He is, I would think He would be happy to let you remain in the meadow to munch on your grass and grow fat. Maybe He isn't so nice after all. Or maybe He isn't even paying attention? What do you think, Little Lamb?"

"What a waste," Edgar spat out. "Your God is no more powerful than you are. He is an imaginary hope for mindless, hopeless creatures."

Again Edgar waited for an answer. He didn't mind waiting. The sun was shining through the wispy mist that comprised his vision; the wind was softly blowing. It was a good day for an argument. It was turning out to be a one-sided one, but that never stopped Edgar. It simply made it more of a game, for Edgar knew how to claw and pick with the sharp talons of his words, deeper and deeper until he found a raw nerve. Sooner or later he would get there. And when he found that nerve, he would peck at it as persistently and painfully as he could.

That's the way his game was usually played. And yet it was a bit different with Galya. In all the time he had known the sheep, he had never quite gotten the better of him. Galya could be irritated. Galya would argue. But the sheep had never given in to anger or tears. This was what fascinated the raven. Galya seemed to treat him as a friend. What a strange little sheep he was!

For his part, Galya thought it was all a bit strange, too. The bitter raven could be almost unbearable company in the best of times. But Galya knew that Edgar wasn't so much mean as he was angry and hurt. Everyone had the right to feel angry and hurt—even if they felt that way a bit more often than most animals. And Galya knew that Edgar was curious about him, fascinated with him, wondering why he was happy and content. The sheep insisted on hope; the raven insisted on bitterness.

"Give it up, Edgar." Galya said the words finally, and the raven twitched in surprise.

It was as fierce a response as Edgar was going to get. Galya couldn't see much of a point in having the usual argument with a bird who was blind in more ways than one. They had been through it all before—too many times, in fact. Edgar seemed determined to hash over their differences on the subject of the Creator of all things. He would make some pointed remark, calculated to draw a response; Galya would offer a mild retort. The exchange would gradually ascend to the level of an argument, rising a few degrees in heat with every reply. Finally the bird would flap away in rage and bewilderment—only to raise the subject again at the first opportunity. Why was this the one subject he insisted on battling over?

Well, not today—not today of all days. Galya had problems to face, and an argument about the Maker of the animals carried no appeal at all. He still trusted the Maker, but yes, he had questions of his own about what was being demanded of him. Why must he give his life? Before today, he hadn't thought to wonder about why these shepherds might need a sacrifice. But now the question had a whole new feel to it.

Galya needed time to think—and it looked as though he would have that time. Since the men had brought him to the new pen, they

had been constantly fussing over him. He was
washed and fed and combed and given plenty
of fresh water. He already knew the sacrifice meant never seeing his home again, but
it was also about being clean and perfect.
Between these times when the men would
hurry out to tend to his needs, Galya had
nothing to do but rotate his thoughts
around in his mind. And most of these
thoughts revolved around his Maker, and
what it meant to be a sacrifice and to be
clean and perfect.

A cough intruded on his thoughts, and
Galya looked up. The old raven was still there, apparently waiting for
a reply or a rebuff of some kind. "I'd rather be alone," Galya offered,
not unkindly.

"Oh, you'll get your wish. You're going to be more alone than
you've ever been in your whole woolly life!" chuckled Edgar darkly.

Edgar flapped his wings twice before leaping into the air. Galya
almost called out to him, but Edgar had vanished with the wind.
Even now, even deluged with worries of his own, Galya felt the need
to offer some word of hope to his miserable and embittered friend—
some ray of light. Maybe it was the last opportunity he would have
to do such a thing, for Edgar or for anybody else.

The Sheep Tales

While Galya slept, the men brought more food. With a yawn, the
sheep stumbled to his feet and ate his fill, then he found a warm
place in the sun and lay down again. He thought back over his life.
He thought about the faces of his friends and his family. And he
thought of the Sheep Tales—despite everything that had happened,
these tales brought Galya a smile. He smiled as he thought of all
the stories that had come down to him.

The tales were all about animals, but they were really about the
Maker of the animals. The Maker must love the many creatures of

the earth, for He had often allowed them to play a part in the great things He was doing in the world. Imagine that—a Maker who would demonstrate His power by using simple animals.

The tales were all about that, and Galya had heard them all. Men could read and write, and they sometimes kept the stories on rustling parchment. The animals couldn't read, but they could hear and remember. They passed along the stories, one beast to another, until the woods crackled with the tales told and retold in every creature's own style, from lion right down to ladybug.

The stories made Galya laugh, and sometimes they made him cry. And he wondered if now, by some amazing stroke of fate, he would take his place in these tales. Even if it ended up being a story that would make an animal cry, this thought gave him hope, for the stories always had a lesson and a meaning to them. And as much as Galya did not want to die, perhaps the meaning of the stories was that Galya's sacrifice, too, would be turned into something wonderful for God.

As the days passed, each was little different from the one before it—food and water, cleaning and grooming, thinking and sleeping. Galya lay in the warm sun and told himself the Sheep Tales. If his mother and father had been here, or his dearest friends, he knew that's what *they* would do, for the Sheep Tales bring comfort and strength. As each story began and ended, he felt a growing peace and even contentment, despite knowing that he was fast approaching the time of the sacrifice.

The peace came from the "big idea" that flowed through all the stories—the big idea that he would not die to become someone's meal or clothing; he would die to provide a *service*—a very important one. *This* was what the sheep meant when they spoke of honor and pride in the sacrifice. Galya could see why they held their shoulders a bit higher and spoke with a hint of joy when they talked about members of their family who had become the sacrifice. The tales made it abundantly clear that his blood would provide something for all of creation that could not be provided in any other way.

This was a mystery, surely, but he knew that the spilling of his blood was a grand thing—the finest and best service he could ever perform. Of course, he would miss the simple pleasures of life, but something inside of him told him to be strong and not to be anxious.

On the third day Edgar returned. "Ah, but aren't we looking fat and juicy today?" he snickered. He had looked forward to using those clever words.

Galya laughed pleasantly in reply. It startled Edgar so much that he almost catapulted from his perch. It was both irritating and curious—who would laugh at such a cruel jest about himself?

"What's so funny?" rasped Edgar, who did not at all appreciate being the brunt of a joke.

Galya laughed again, harder this time. He was in a chattier mood today. "I don't mean to laugh at you, Edgar, but since we last talked I've been going over my favorite stories—the Sheep Tales. And you remind me of some of the characters in the stories. One of those characters even said, 'What's so funny?' exactly like you just did."

Edgar sniffed indignantly. "Little Lamb, I am nothing like those foolish tales. Nothing at all. I still don't see what is so funny."

"Forgive me, my friend, but *you* are what is so funny, Edgar. You make your little jokes, but you miss the point. The Sheep Tales helped me see this. It turns out that I'm not the one who should be feeling miserable at all. You see, I have discovered a ray of hope in the midst of all this. . ." Galya paused, trying to think of the right word.

"Bird dung!" Edgar harrumphed. And Galya laughed again. He had never seen the bird taken so completely aback. It was impossible to be upset with Edgar, because the look on his face was so amusing!

"Bird dung indeed, Edgar," Galya smiled. "Sometimes it takes a little dung to understand being clean, and a little darkness to see how beautiful the light can be. I wish you could see that there is so much more than dung and darkness. But if a sky full of blessings were to fall on you, Edgar, you still wouldn't see it. You would complain that it made a bump on your feathery head. You wouldn't enjoy my stories, my friend, because they are filled with hope and

"Tell me the stories," he demanded, hopping down from his perch and settling into a warm patch of dirt in the sun.

your heart is more blinded to the hope of this world than your eyes are to the light of this world."

These words had poured out of Galya so quickly that he was as startled as Edgar. Where had all of it come from? Perhaps he had needed to face his own moment of truth before he could know how to face the ridicule of a raven.

For a moment or two, there was silence between the old friends. Then Edgar spoke up. "Tell me the stories," he demanded, hopping down from his perch and settling into a warm patch of dirt in the sun. "Show me what is so funny, and let me be the judge."

Galya couldn't believe his ears. Oh, they had been through their arguments; they had gone round and round. But it was so rare that Edgar wanted to listen. He liked to be the one doing all the talking. Now he actually wanted to listen to the stories—or so he said. Perhaps he would question every little bit of the narrative, and throw in nasty and sarcastic remarks to boot. Who could say? Galya only knew he now had a chance to tell the Sheep Tales, and he loved doing so.

Edgar rolled his sightless eyes as Galya began: "These are the stories that hold the mysterious key of hope that will last long after you and I are gone."

"You'll be gone a lot sooner than I will," Edgar muttered, pretending to be looking away. But Galya knew he was listening, so he began with the first and the oldest of all the tales.

Paradise Lost

In the beginning God created the heavens and the earth. Now the earth was formless and empty, darkness was over the surface of the deep, and the Spirit of God was hovering over the waters.

And God said, "Let there be light," and there was light.[1]

ARVID

Arvid opened his eyes, turned around slowly, and wondered exactly where he was.

Colors—that's what he noticed first. The colors took his breath away. Lush greens of every shade rippled and waved as near as his toes and as distant as the misty horizon. But there were other colors, too—browns and yellows and oranges, not to mention the delightful clusters of bright flowers. All Arvid could do was whisper one word over and over: "Beautiful! Beautiful!" He was living within a wonderful dream, if he was indeed awake—and he felt very, very awake.

Arvid squinted into the sky. Above him hung a brilliant blue canopy as wide as forever, embellished by billowing white wonders taking part in a slow, unhurried dance from one horizon to the other. Arvid inhaled a deep, refreshing breath of air. He tasted the cool flavor of the breeze after a summer storm has scrubbed the world clean. He took another breath and closed his eyes to savor it within him.

Suddenly Arvid heard chuckling and then giggling, and he realized his foot was being tickled. He looked down to see that he had stepped into the shallows of a stream, and its tiny waves were dancing playfully among his toes. The waters seemed to be laughing at his intrusion.

The sights, the smells, the touch, the sounds, even the taste of the wind and the mist were all pure and clean and perfect—all a gift from some wonderful Someone. Even Arvid's mind was clean. There were no memories, no anxious thoughts—only the place, the moment, and the wonder in which he found himself. The where and the why didn't seem important for right now—not even the *whom!* For if you had asked him his name or his favorite things to do, you would have received only a smile and a shrug.

All that was important to Arvid was that everything was pure and new. Anything could happen, and especially anything wonderful. His history was a mystery and his future held no clue. But he knew he belonged here, and he knew that the great task before him was to explore, to discover, and to enjoy.

Then there was the sound. As he took in the beauty around him, he heard something that caused him to gasp. He recognized the sound as a voice, and the voice as a whisper, and the whisper as a word—one word that unleashed a clamor of laughter and applause. The sound was so joyful and so thrilling that Arvid suddenly wanted nothing more in life than to be a part of it. The waters of the stream seemed to be babbling with excitement as they hurried somewhere. Maybe they would lead him to the laughter. He slid into the water, and the cool stream led him along with breathless little splashes of excitement. Arvid felt the joy of moving and of feeling the spray, the thrill of anticipation and discovery.

The greens and browns of Arvid's new home rushed by him, and soon they gave way to a vast, sunny meadow. The great clearing was bright enough to make one blink, but in its very center something was shining with such intensity that other things practically faded into shadows beside its radiance.

Somehow Arvid knew he had found the Source of the deep skies and billowy clouds, the lush greens and the laughing waters. Here, before his very eyes, was the living Fountain of light from which every good thing rippled into life. He found himself part of the laughter and applause. Joy and praise seemed to leap from his heart to embrace the great living, laughing Source of the light.

All around the Bright One were lesser lights—sparkling ones that were beautiful indeed, but they only called attention to the One they served. They were something like stardust in all the colors of the rainbow and some too beautiful and bright to be found even there; they were weaving and cascading in a dance and a song that celebrated creation.

Arvid could not have removed his eyes from the spectacle for anything in the world. The Bright One was moving about, hesitating for the flicker of an instant to whisper a name, then moving on. With each wonderful whisper, the great crowd of creatures would stop, drink in the new word freshly spoken, and explode in laughter and applause as that word literally burst into life. For suddenly where there had been only expectant emptiness, the newest word

exploded colorfully into fur and feather and flesh. It would then bound about the meadow on four feet, or skitter away on many legs, or soar into the blue sky on two wings— and the newness and beauty of the sight brought fresh gasps of wonder and amazement every time.

Each new creature, after recovering from the shock of entry into life, finally stepped into the growing circle of celebration. And with each new addition, the sparkling creatures added a new movement to their dance and a new verse to their song.

So much breathtaking variety! A new creature would move about in its own perfect rhythm and style, then it would sound off with the kind of voice perfectly suited to it. There would be a roar or a call or a bray or a whistling song, but it was always something just right. Some of the creatures were silent, but even then their silence was their song, and they too took part in the great meadow celebration. Arvid saw that the circle was growing to a great throng, as ring after ring of new arrivals joined the circle.

Then the Bright One whispered again. And the word He spoke sounded something like—"Elephant!"

You see, these were all words spoken in the Language of the Bright One. Later, the Maker would allow His first man to name the animals for himself. And *Elephant* was the name that man used, and the name we use when we tell this tale—for the Language of the Light, as we shall sadly see, was lost to the creatures of the earth not long after this.

So the word rang out—"Elephant!" And out of the blue, like a thunderclap made entirely of color and music, a great empty place before the Maker was filled up with the most wonderful creature. This was Elephant, a beast as regal and fanciful as his name.

Arvid thought, *The Bright One must have been overflowing with laughter and artistry when He spoke this one into being*—for Elephant's look was strikingly different from any other new creature. His ears were bigger than Arvid's entire body. Elephant moved with a rambling, rumbling step as graceful as it was massive. He had a long, gorgeous nose that swung right and left, right and left, as if to say, "Here comes Elephant! Make way for Elephant!"

On the moment he appeared, Elephant raised his nose and trumpeted his ecstasy at being alive. As Arvid watched, time stood still—for time, like everything else, was also watching the wonderful show.

"Cow . . . Frog . . . Monkey . . . Duck." Each new arrival seemed more magnificent or surprising or humorous or fascinating than the last. Each had never previously been seen or imagined. Creativity reigned supreme and unrestrained. Arvid felt highly fortunate to have been invited to such an event.

But as he thought about it, he began to realize that he wasn't a guest in the meadow by chance; he was a part of the occasion! Like all the other creatures, he was fresh and new. This was why he didn't know his name. This was why he could remember no "yesterday."

For the first time, Arvid became completely aware of his own body. He looked down and saw wonderful webbed feet. No wonder he had felt so natural in the stream, and no wonder the waters were laughing and welcoming him! He craned his neck and discovered a sleek body covered with lovely fur. Hints of brown and red glistened in the sunlight. Suddenly he wanted badly to see his face. But no matter how hard he tried or how much he twisted, he couldn't see it.

Then he thought of the stream. He had passed a quiet place where he had caught a brief glimpse of another creature. In his eagerness, he hadn't stopped to investigate the mysterious creature—this one seemed to be in a hurry, too. But he remembered its beauty and elegance. For some reason, that creature seemed like one he could talk to; maybe it would still be dwelling by the water, and maybe Arvid could ask it to look him over and describe his appearance.

But when Arvid came to the quiet spot in the stream, the creature was no longer there.

Perhaps he was hiding; perhaps he had slipped down beneath the surface. Arvid moved to the edge of the bank and looked into the water. His eyes widened with wonder. He was right! There was his friend, looking right back at him! *What a lovely, graceful*—thing, Arvid thought. For he didn't know its name. He moved closer to introduce himself, and the creature in the water moved closer too.

He stared at the creature in fascination, and the creature stared right back. Arvid opened his mouth to speak, but suddenly he realized he didn't know what to say. How could he introduce himself? He had no name. He turned away, and as he did so, the creature in the water turned away too, with the same look of confusion. That was odd. Arvid stole a peek at his counterpart from the corner of his eye. His friend was peeking too! Arvid's mouth dropped open in surprise, as did the other mouth.

Then Arvid began to laugh. He buried his face and laughed until he cried. Arvid had suddenly recognized the same beautiful fur and webbed feet, and he understood that the little mirrored pool of water was making a perfect picture of him so that he could see what he looked like. What a friendly world this was!

Arvid looked carefully at the water, and he began to smile. He was just as handsome and unique as any animal he had seen. And his name ...

Yes—it all came back to him in a rush of memories. Arvid remembered his first sensation in the world. He had heard the words *Duck-Billed Platypus.* What marvelous words! How could he have forgotten them? He had forgotten them because he had swooned with the excitement of his first glimpse at the world—and at the sight of the Bright One who had whispered him into life with a smile. This was more excitement than a Duck-Billed Platypus could handle, and he had fainted. How strange!

Now, of course, he was grateful to have solved the mystery and to know that he was just as fine and special as all the other wonderful creatures. He was pleased with his delicate fur and his handy webbed feet. But most of all, he was proud to know he had been made by such a kind and loving World-Maker, whose perfection brought life and wonder everywhere he walked.

"I am gorgeous, gorgeous, perfectly *gorgeous!*" Arvid shouted as he plunged joyfully into the water, scattering his image in a million sparkling droplets.

It was exhilarating to be alive.

•   •   •

Edgar was chuckling darkly. "Have you ever seen a duck-billed platypus?" he challenged. "They look like they were designed by a committee. If this Arvid thought he was beautiful, he was blinder than I," Edgar sniffed, as if to dismiss the whole tale with a flick of his beak.

Galya loved Arvid's story, but Edgar had been shaking his head slowly back and forth with each new detail; now he couldn't hold back his disdain. Galya smiled patiently, for at least Edgar had listened quietly for most of the story—unusual for him. And his protest actually gave the sheep an opportunity to make an important point. "Everything was good and beautiful in the beginning," he explained. After each new creation the Great Book says over and over again, "God saw that it was good."

Edgar was strutting back and forth along his perch, ruffling his feathers. "Let me see if I understand this, Little Lamb. This 'Bright One' goes around whispering! He must be whispering because He's embarrassed by His work. After all, what good is a duck with no feathers? Maybe the Bright One isn't so bright after all. And what about that awkward, ugly name—*Duck-Billed Platypus*? *Raven*—now there's a fine name, short and snappy! No nonsense about it. When I introduce myself, my name commands respect. By the time your platypus finishes saying *his* entire name, everyone has gone home. Ha!" Edgar was always pleased with his jokes (and he was used to being the only one laughing at them).

"In the long-ago times, people didn't look at things so bleakly," Galya said quietly. "In the beginning, everything was beautiful."

"What changed?" Edgar snapped.

"Listen to the rest of the story. I expect you'll find the answer to that question, and many others," Galya answered. "Unless, of course, you're not curious to find out what happened next."

Edgar spat contemptuously and let out a rather nasty "Squawk," but he didn't fly away. Galya continued his story.

● ● ●

Friends

Arvid was quite pleased with the way things were working out, and he sighed deeply with happiness. But as he paused to take it all in, he discovered a new thing called *weariness*. He had run fresh out of energy. Arvid hunkered down to the soft bank of the stream and closed his eyes. And he was just on the verge of a second new discovery—the thing known as a *nap*—when the ground around him began quite suddenly to tremble. Startled, Arvid opened his eyes to see the whole abundant width, height, and depth of Elephant looming over him.

Elephant had come down to the stream to drink, and his footsteps were not what we would call light or gentle. Arvid watched in amazement as Elephant drank water in a way a platypus could never have imagined; he sucked gallons of liquid into his great, wriggling nose before squirting the drink from his nose into his mouth. Arvid smiled a great duck-billed smile to see such a curious sight. When Elephant had drunk his fill, he turned to make his lumbering way back to the meadow. Arvid fell in step beside him, and they chatted pleasantly as they walked.

When the two creatures arrived at the great wide meadow, the sun was sinking beneath the distant hills, painting the sky in radiant reds and oranges. The animals were content to sit quietly and enjoy the novelty of their first sunset. But there was something else; the animals seemed to be waiting for a new event.

Arvid noticed for the first time how many birds filled the branches of the trees and hopped along the blades of grass. And thousands of other magnificent aviators circled above, silhouetted against the lovely sky. As Arvid and Elephant moved closer, a raven landed on the very crown of Elephant's head. "Hurry, please!" urged the raven. "You'll miss it!"

• • •

"A raven? Did you say a raven?" Edgar interjected, suddenly more interested.

"Yes, you heard correctly," Galya smiled, and resumed the story.

• • •

The voice of the Bright One broke the silence. No whisper this time. His voice boomed like thunder, shook the trees, and rebounded from the distant hills.

"Let us make man in our image, in our likeness," He said, "and let them rule over the fish of the sea and the birds of the air, over the livestock, over all the earth, and over all the creatures that move along the ground."

The sparkling ones broke into applause at these words, and they began a new song. The raven screeched in delight and flew close to the Bright One, beckoning Elephant and Arvid to join him. When they arrived, the raven resumed his perch atop Elephant's head, where he could get the best possible view.

The Bright One scooped His hands into the warm earth and brought them out again, caressing the dirt in His hands as though it were precious jewelry. Then, with a flourish, He threw the dusty powder into the air. The animals waited for it to settle back to the ground, but this never happened. With a deafening clap of thunder, the hovering dust sparkled momentarily and then snapped into a shape. There was a gasp all across the meadow, for the form was a vivid likeness of the Bright One Himself! Was there no end to the surprises?

Slowly the animals moved forward to inspect the replica of their Creator. The birds hovered as closely as they dared. Elephant extended a tentative nose forward to touch the new creature. It must have tickled, for the new creature smiled. And with that, the meadow shook with the applause and laughter of the great assembly. All of the earlier celebration couldn't match what came to pass now, for the smile on the new creature was the very likeness of the Bright One Himself.

The sparkling ones sang for joy, the birds flew in exquisite patterns, the monkeys swung wildly through the trees, and horses galloped through the meadow. The Bright One smiled so broadly that for a moment the meadow was brighter than noon. He threw back His head in jolly laughter, and the ground shook so hard that even Elephant nearly toppled over.

> So God created man in his own image,
>> in the image of God he created him;
>> male and female he created them.

God blessed them and said to them, "Be fruitful and increase in number; fill the earth and subdue it. Rule over the fish of the sea and the birds of the air and over every living creature that moves on the ground."

Then God said, "I give you every seed-bearing plant on the face of the whole earth and every tree that has fruit with seed in it. They will be yours for food. And to all the beasts of the earth and all the birds of the air and all the creatures that move on the ground—everything that has the breath of life in it—I give every green plant for food." And it was so.

God saw all that he had made, and it was very good. And there was evening, and there was morning—the sixth day.[2]

Elephant and Raven and Arvid settled down close together that night, and they drifted off to sleep chattering about all the amazing things they had seen that day. Their slumber was deep and refreshing, filled with dreams—though no dream could surpass the true events they had witnessed. In the middle of the night, Arvid spoke in his sleep. He kept murmuring, "It is good. It is good. It is all so very good."

Even the Bright One rested. In the entire universe, from the most distant star to the newest butterfly, all was good.

Elephant and Arvid became close friends. There was so much to explore. They laughed until the tears came on the day of the river bath, when something quite unexpected happened. Elephant stepped into water a bit too deep even for him. He was an excellent swimmer, but this was a swift river. The current unexpectedly swept Elephant off his feet. Head over heels, his huge body tossed and tumbled in the turbulent water. A leg would appear, then a foot, then a huge gray bottom with a ropy tale. Finally nothing but Elephant's nose protruded from the surface of the water like a huge sea snake.

Arvid ran along the bank to keep pace, but a platypus hasn't the best feet for running. He bumped into trees, tripped over a rock, and fell into the water. He was laughing so hard he choked and had to swim quickly to the surface to fill his lungs with air. Then, with a chuckle, bubbles still streaming from his bill, he caught up with his friend.

He was an excellent swimmer, but this was a swift river. The current unexpectedly swept Elephant off his feet. Head over heels, his huge body tossed and tumbled in the turbulent water.

Elephant finally latched on to a tree branch as he passed, and he managed to pull himself from the river, quivering with laugher and shooting a spray of water from his nose. The two friends lay beside the river to catch their breath, then to laugh over Elephant's mishap. They couldn't stop. Just when they thought they were fresh out of giggles, one of them would describe the ridiculous picture again—an elephant sailing down a river—and they would start howling all over again.

From that day on, Arvid called elephant Sub, and they became inseparable friends.

> Now the LORD God had planted a garden in the east, in Eden; and there he put the man he had formed. And the LORD God made all kinds of trees grow out of the ground—trees that were pleasing to the eye and good for food. In the middle of the garden were the tree of life and the tree of the knowledge of good and evil. . . .
>
> The LORD God took the man and put him in the Garden of Eden to work it and take care of it. And the LORD God commanded the man, "You are free to eat from any tree in the garden; but you must not eat from the tree of the knowledge of good and evil, for when you eat of it you will surely die."[3]

Arvid and Sub enjoyed their wanderings. Every setting they discovered was beautiful and pleasing in some new way. But one day they came to a place that seemed to be the Bright One's masterpiece. It was a garden, and the two creatures were so astonished to drink in the loveliness of the trees and fruits and flowers that they could not speak. Their chatter broke off abruptly.

The colors were so beautiful they almost hurt the eye. The cold crystal springs bubbled their welcome. Trees joyfully lifted their stout, curling branches to the heavens, forming a canopy of greenery to provide cool shade in the midday sun.

In the midst of it all was the beautiful child of the Bright One, happily gathering fruit and flowers. He looked up to see his two visitors. He seemed very pleased and surprised. "I don't believe we've met," he said. "I am Man. But I haven't given you names yet, have I?"

The man peered at each of them for an intent moment, then he gave them the names you and I already knew—*Elephant* and *Duck-Billed Platypus*. After offering each name, he grinned with pleasure.

This was the first time Arvid and Sub had heard their names in the language of men, and they smiled as much as the man did. They just seemed to fit so well. *El–e–phant. Duck-Billed Plat–y–pus. Sub and Arvid.*

The two friends could not bring themselves to leave the garden. It was like living within a dream, a feast for the eyes and fragrances for the nose and delicious things for the stomach.

As the moon rose each evening, they would lie awake to watch the stars blink at them. During the day they enjoyed exploring the garden together. You would never have guessed that two animals who looked so different from each other would be so devoted in friendship, but their differences were never a problem. Sub could reach the higher leaves of a tree while Arvid couldn't, but that was all right; Arvid had little interest in eating leaves. Sub, for his part, had no desire to eat the little insects that Arvid was much better at uncovering. Arvid was a graceful and swift swimmer, but Sub could walk for days on dry land without tiring.

One starlit night the two of them were enjoying another belly laugh about the day Sub took his river journey when they heard a voice that was new to them.

"What's so funny?" asked the voice.

• • •

Edgar had closed his eyes, but now he jerked them open. "Ah!" he called out in triumph. "This will be the character you said I reminded you of when I spoke those very words—'what's so funny?'"

Galya nodded and continued.

A Stranger in Paradise

"What's so funny?"

Something about the manner of these three words made Arvid's blood run cold. The voice had the lifeless sound of one who was

"We've never met," said Arvid politely but a bit nervously. "What is your name?

"I have many names," the creature sneered. "You may call me Wise. But I believe
asked you a question. What is so funny?"

incapable of experiencing laughter. Arvid and Sub looked around them and there, in the moonlight, was the silhouette of a beautiful creature, thin and elegant, with a graceful way of moving. Narrow, intense eyes seemed to cut through the darkness to regard them curiously—and the stranger's presence seemed to cast a chill in the air.

"We've never met," said Arvid politely but a bit nervously. "What is your name?"

"I have many names," the creature sneered. "You may call me Wise. But I believe I asked you a question. What is so funny?"

Arvid tried to tell about the river and Sub's adventure in it. But his words didn't seem to flow as easily as they had before, and he couldn't seem to express the humor of the sight of the elephant bobbing in the rapids. The sinister stranger sat very deep in the shadows of the tree as Arvid spoke, glaring at the speaker. Arvid was relieved to finally reach the end of his story. When he finished, there was no response from the creature other than a bored sigh and a slimy, sickening sound like someone chewing with his mouth open or smacking his lips to wet a dry and sticky tongue.

All the laughter and calmness had drained out of the air. After a few uncomfortable moments of silence, Arvid tried to lighten the mood by recalling the day of the great celebration in the meadow, when all the animals came to life at the speaking of their names. Then he talked about how he and Sub had come to be friends, and how they had discovered the different talents they had. But Arvid's words finally trailed off into a bewildered stammer.

The serpent—for the strange creature, of course, was a serpent—looked at Arvid, his eyes narrowing to mere slits, and said, "Why do you have the bill of a duck if you are not a duck?"

Arvid had never even thought about such a thing. Before he could frame a reply, the intruder added another question: "Can you fly like a duck?"

Arvid was confused. He had never thought to compare himself with another creature—weren't all living things unique and beautiful? The stars seemed dimmer now, and the chill was becoming stronger. Only moments before it had been just another evening of blissful contentment. Sub, who had been trembling since the stranger had first spoken, now climbed to his great, oaklike feet. He gently nudged Arvid with his nose and whispered, "I believe we have someplace else to go."

But Arvid didn't seem to hear. He was looking intently at the stranger. And the stranger was watching him, too.

"Pardon me, I didn't realize you and your friend thought yourselves to be beautiful," said the serpent, with a crooked little smirk. "Do you really think you are beautiful?"

With that, Sub wrapped his nose completely around his smaller friend, lifted him off the ground, and trudged heavily into the forest, away from the humorless creature. In all their short days, neither Arvid nor Sub had ever experienced anything like this. It was as if someone had planted a terrible seed in the middle of the beautiful garden. And the strange creature had planted a terrible seed in the hearts of Arvid and Sub. Sub broke into a lumbering run and smiled as he heard Arvid grunt with each step. Nothing had been lost yet. The seed had not sprouted. The abundance of light and life and beauty had overwhelmed its presence.

Yet there was a dull ache that came just from knowing the seed existed. Finally the air grew warm again, and they found an exquisite place to rest. Sub gently lowered Arvid to the ground. A merciful peace kept their minds from dwelling on the slithering questions the creature had asked. They spoke of happy things as they drifted into slumber, so that their dreams would be the nice kind they had come to expect. During the night, Sub woke up. He heard Arvid tossing restlessly and murmuring, "I am beautiful, I am beautiful, I am."

"Yes, you are!" Sub chuckled softly as he closed his eyes again.

But the kind elephant wouldn't have smiled if those eyes could have seen even just a little bit into the future. He wouldn't have smiled at all to know that even now, as his friend tossed restlessly in his sleep, the seeds sown by the creature were taking root in the midst of the unspoiled beauty that surrounded them.

Now the serpent was more crafty than any of the wild animals the LORD God had made. He said to the woman, "Did God really say, 'You must not eat from any tree in the garden'?"

The woman said to the serpent, "We may eat fruit from the trees in the garden, but God did say, 'You must not eat fruit from the tree that is in the middle of the garden, and you must not touch it, or you will die.'"

"You will not surely die," the serpent said to the woman. "For God knows that when you eat of it your eyes will be opened, and you will be like God, knowing good and evil."

When the woman saw that the fruit of the tree was good for food and pleasing to the eye, and also desirable for gaining wisdom, she took some and ate it. She also gave some to her husband, who was with her, and he ate it. Then the eyes of both of them were opened, and they realized they were naked; so they sewed fig leaves together and made coverings for themselves.

Then the man and his wife heard the sound of the LORD God as he was walking in the garden in the cool of the day, and they hid from the LORD God among the trees of the garden. But the LORD God called to the man, "Where are you?"

He answered, "I heard you in the garden, and I was afraid because I was naked; so I hid."

And he said, "Who told you that you were naked? Have you eaten from the tree that I commanded you not to eat from?"

The man said, "The woman you put here with me—she gave me some fruit from the tree, and I ate it."

Then the LORD God said to the woman, "What is this you have done?"

The woman said, "The serpent deceived me, and I ate."[4]

• • •

The story about the stranger seemed to upset Edgar. He paced up and down his perch as he listened. Something was on his mind. Galya stopped speaking for a moment to give the raven a chance to have his say.

"Interesting," he said. "Of all the beautiful animals you took pains to describe, there is only one who is unpleasant. And that's the one I remind you of! What a friend *you* are."

Galya replied, "Edgar, it's just that you and the stranger both used the words, 'What's so funny?' And since you raised the subject, didn't I hear you mocking the duck-billed platypus a few moments ago, just as the serpent did?"

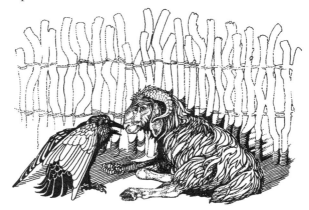

Edgar muttered under his breath, and Galya laughed. "Don't worry, Edgar. I wouldn't quite put you on a level with the serpent, but you must admit—you do share his point of view."

Edgar pushed his beak right up to Galya's nose. "Well, then, let's put it this way," he said. "The serpent and I are both very wise, and we have no time for foolishness and sentiment." The raven barked out the words, but Galya didn't completely believe he meant them.

Edgar was pacing again, while Galya observed him quietly. "Well," said the raven, "proceed—if you've got any story left! Proceed!" And Galya concluded the first Sheep Tale.

•   •   •

The garden was buzzing with the news. It was a disaster; it was unthinkable.

When Arvid and Sub heard the news about the fruit, the tree, and the children of the Bright One, they felt very ill deep down. Before they were even told, they knew the serpent was at the heart of the tragic events surrounding the ones called Adam and Eve.

Why, the thing had happened at the very tree where Arvid and Sub had begun to sleep the night before. Everyone knew the fruit of that tree was untouchable. The Bright One had clearly forbidden it, and He had been clear about the consequences of disobedience—namely, death. Yet the serpent had managed to convince the man and the woman to ignore the clear instructions. The same voice that had first hissed, "What's so funny?" and "Do you really think you are beautiful?" had later said, "You will *not* surely die." The two animal friends could hear the voice in their minds, and the same spooky chill returned.

Sorrow fell like a great blanket across the garden. By their act of disobedience, the man and the woman had let darkness and death into their perfect paradise. Nothing was quite the same now. The man and the woman had been sent away, and one of the Bright One's brilliant servants now guarded the entrance with a flaming sword. And the whispers of the night revealed that no one was sadder than the Bright One. The man and the woman were His special children; they had been created to bear His likeness. And now He wept over losing the closeness of the friendship they had enjoyed.

Arvid and Sub found the garden too sad a place to stay now, after the serpent had done his dastardly deed. Late in the day they made their way out, hoping to find some of the places they had known and loved earlier. Even though it was night, they saw a glow in the south, where the servant with the flaming sword stood guard. They went out of their way to avoid that place and finally settled down not far from where the man slept.

Late in the night, they heard a familiar voice—the man, Adam, crying out in misery. "Please don't leave us alone, Lord!" he wept. "Please help us!" It was almost more than Arvid and Sub could bear, and sleep did not come easily that night. Questions, on the other hand, came in abundance. Arvid spoke up. "Has the Bright One abandoned His children now? Has He abandoned us?"

After a long silence, Sub heaved a huge sigh and answered, "I don't know." After another long silence, broken only by the chirp of crickets and the moan of a soft wind, Sub said, "All we have is hope, Arvid."

But Arvid didn't dream of hope—only of the serpent and the angel and flaming swords. His fitful cries woke Sub: "Please don't leave us! Please don't leave us."

Sub gently touched Arvid with his long nose and added his own plea. "Yes, Lord, please help us," he said.

And the great elephant closed his eyes and wondered what lay ahead.

● ● ●

Edgar began pacing back and forth, waiting for more story, but Galya had finished. "And that's your ending?" Edgar asked incredulously. "Are you serious? Now *there's* a story to brighten your day. The Maker of all loses control! He allows everything to be fouled up! And this is the Creator you're so excited about?"

"He lost control of nothing," Galya responded firmly. "He let the man and woman decide what to do, and they made the worst choice possible."

"Either way, fouled up is fouled up," sneered Edgar. "All I get out of your story is that your world and mine stinks! If I'm going to spend my valuable time listening to your stories, you'll have to do much better than that."

Galya could feel the blood rising in his face, but his voice was calm as he spoke. "You have to hear *all* the Sheep Tales, Edgar. I agree with you, this one is very sad. It explains why we face problems in this world. But it's only the beginning. There's much more."

Galya paused, fully expecting Edgar to fly away. He could see that his friend was agitated. But Edgar only sighed in exasperation. He stared at Galya impatiently through his cloudy eyes, waiting for the next story. As it began, he continued pacing.

The Lion's Tale

There were so many stories Galya could tell, and he could think of many that might help Edgar understand the sad condition of the world. But Edgar had been so disturbed by the sad ending to the story of creation that Galya chose to share a story about the mighty power of God.

This tale had been passed down by one of the most feared and respected creatures from the entire animal kingdom, so perhaps Edgar would listen more willingly. Maybe the story of Dandy would help Edgar see the truth.

DANDY LION

Now Daniel so distinguished himself among the administrators and the satraps by his exceptional qualities that the king planned to set him over the whole kingdom. At this, the administrators and the satraps tried to find grounds for charges against Daniel in his conduct of government affairs, but they were unable to do so. They could find no corruption in him, because he was trustworthy and neither corrupt nor negligent. Finally these men said, "We will never find any basis for charges against this man Daniel unless it has something to do with the law of his God."

So the administrators and the satraps went as a group to the king and said: "O King Darius, live forever! The royal administrators, prefects, satraps, advisers and governors have all agreed that the king should issue an edict and enforce the decree that anyone who prays to any god or man during the next thirty days, except to you, O king, shall be thrown into the lions' den. Now, O king, issue the decree and put it in writing so that it cannot be altered—in accordance with the laws of the Medes and Persians, which cannot be repealed." So King Darius put the decree in writing.

Now when Daniel learned that the decree had been published, he went home to his upstairs room where the windows opened toward Jerusalem. Three times a day he got down on his knees and prayed, giving thanks to his God, just as he had done before. Then these men went as a group and found Daniel praying and asking God for help. So they went to the king and spoke to him about his royal decree: "Did you not publish a decree that during the next thirty days anyone who prays to any god or man except to you, O king, would be thrown into the lions' den?"

The king answered, "The decree stands—in accordance with the laws of the Medes and Persians, which cannot be repealed."

Then they said to the king, "Daniel, who is one of the exiles from Judah, pays no attention to you, O king, or to the decree you put in writing. He still prays three times a day." When the king heard this, he was greatly distressed; he was determined to rescue Daniel and made every effort until sundown to save him.

Then the men went as a group to the king and said to him, "Remember, O king, that according to the law of the Medes and Persians no decree or edict that the king issues can be changed."

So the king gave the order, and they brought Daniel and threw him into the lions' den. The king said to Daniel, "May your God, whom you serve continually, rescue you!"

A stone was brought and placed over the mouth of the den, and the king sealed it with his own signet ring and with the rings of his nobles, so that Daniel's situation might not be changed. Then the king returned to his palace and spent the night without eating and without any entertainment being brought to him. And he could not sleep.[1]

Dandy lived in an old home—one with quite a history.

Dandy's home had been formed thousands of years earlier, when a river used to flow beneath the mountain. Over time, the churning motion of the water had cut a huge cavern beneath the surface of the earth. From there, the water hurried on through a vast underground river system. Eventually the river headed away in some other direction and disappeared, leaving a cave that had been dry for more time than any animal could remember.

Above the cave, erosion had washed the soil out of a huge group of interlocking boulders, leaving a ragged hole high in the ceiling. Except for a rock embedded near the entrance of the den, the floor of the cave was smooth. The walls extended upward and inward toward the shaft in the ceiling. And down at the bottom—well, that was the place the lions now called home.

The lions couldn't reach the opening, but they enjoyed the light and fresh air that streamed in. Dandy's great-great-grandfather had been one of the first lions to make the cave home. Years ago the king had sealed off all the exits except for the elevated opening where the river had entered the mountain. This was used as an entrance. There were many little passages that led back into the mountain, but the lions rarely ventured there. Over the years the kings had used the cave for two purposes: as a kind of royal zoo, and as a place to dispose of garbage. On the night the man named Daniel came, it had been Dandy's home for three years.

Every day just before noon, the sun would stream through the shaft high in the ceiling. It created a spotlight of warmth that would move slowly across the floor as the day grew older. The lions often fought for the privilege of lying in that wonderful brightness. Not only did they relish the warmth, but they also knew that late in

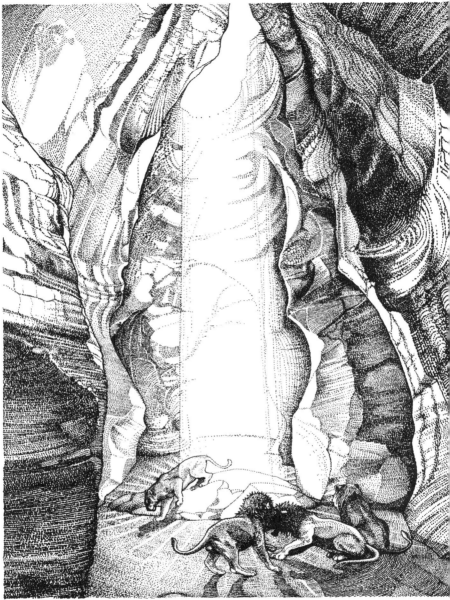

The lions couldn't reach the opening, but they enjoyed the light
and fresh air that streamed in.

the afternoon, when the sunlight touched the smooth stone embedded near the entrance, it would be feeding time. The men from the palace would appear with dinner. It was a first-come, first-serve arrangement. A lion had to be quick to eat.

When the lions heard the sound of voices, the smell of men would begin to filter into the den. The roars of the lions would shake the walls as they fought for position in the patch of light and waited for the food to fall from above. Usually it was leftovers from the palace tables. Sometimes it was a dead or a sickly sheep that men considered unfit for their table. On very rare occasions the meal was even a man! The man might be someone who had attacked the nephew of the king or had broken some law. It didn't matter to the lions whether it was beast or man, dead or alive; whatever entered the den was quickly ripped apart before it touched the floor.

By the time the lions finished fighting over the scraps, the sun had usually moved low enough so that only a sliver of light remained on the floor, then disappeared altogether. For the rest of the evening, the den would be filled with a softening glow until finally darkness claimed the cave. Dandy hated darkness. It was during those dark nights that he most longed for freedom.

He loved the nights when the other light would come. On those nights, somewhere between dusk and dawn, a soft light would come flooding in through the open shaft high in the ceiling. This light did not warm the cave, but it did make his heart feel warm. If he stood in the light and looked up through the opening, Dandy could see a glowing disk suspended in the black night. This was something beautiful for lions to look at, and they were willing to fight each other for a peek at the strange disk. (Then again, lions would fight over almost anything.)

It was on one of those nights when the great disk shone in the night that something happened that Dandy would never forget.

It was a Sunday, Dandy remembered, because on Sundays the lions usually got ribs. He was awakened out of a sound sleep by the murmur of voices. Someone was coming. The light streaming through the hole in the ceiling was brighter than Dandy had ever seen it before. He rushed to the spot where it illuminated the floor. Was it feeding time already?

Still half asleep, Dandy's brain scrambled to make sense out of the confusion. The other lions were just as bewildered as Dandy as they opened their sleepy eyes. They all charged toward the circle of light, their eyes fixed on the opening. The dust they kicked up took on an eerie glow as it boiled through the shaft of evening light. Dandy decided it couldn't be feeding time; the lions were always fed in the daylight, never at night when the special light appeared.

Still, snarling eagerly, Dandy joined the others. Every eye was fixed on the entrance where the shapes of three men appeared out of the darkness. Two of them were pushing and pulling a taller man who walked between them. With an outburst of cursing and laughter, they shoved the taller man through the opening. Dinner would be tasty tonight! Every lion sprang forward as the flailing body fell into the den. These were ribs as fresh as they come.

Dandy was the first to reach the man. He opened his jaws for the first delicious bite—but he couldn't close them. Somehow Dandy's jaws were stuck, wide open.

Although the man lay just inches from Dandy's nose, he couldn't touch him. He lashed out to drag the man toward him, but his claws wouldn't work properly. His paws floundered in thin air as though he were a harmless kitten batting at a ball of string.

Dandy began to tremble with fear and embarrassment. The other lions were watching. He would be teased mercilessly for this. He lunged again, but this time his mouth, which had finally snapped shut, wouldn't open at all! His growls were turned into a deep, throaty hum. Dandy slunk away to a corner of the cave in humiliation. What could be worse than a humming lion?

The meal lay right in the center of the circle of soft light. He was curled into a ball, his hands shielding his head. Dandy glanced around curiously. Amazingly enough, not one of the other lions was tearing at the man either. In his entire life he had never seen *anything* that had entered the den last more than a few seconds. Something very strange was going on.

Sitting beside Dandy was his scarred and scraggly friend, Leopold, the bully of the den. This old warrior would often wait for the other lions to do the killing for him, then seize the parts he wanted. Tonight his eyes were fixed on the meal that lay before him, and his mouth was watering. He cocked his head to one side as he watched the man slowly uncurl. The lions' dinner was very cautiously lowering his arms to take a look around.

A sinister growl rumbled in Leopold's throat as he crouched low and began to twitch. His eyes narrowed to slits and his ears lay flat against his head. But rather than leaping, the old lion could only twitch and slobber. A chuckle escaped from Dandy's throat. He couldn't help himself—here was Leopold the killer lion, the terror of the den, helplessly drooling all over himself. The hunger in his eyes was plain to see, but there was also a look of confusion and apprehension. Dandy didn't dare say anything, for fear that it would come out as a hum again, so he nudged Tawny, the lioness standing next to him.

As Dandy and Tawny chuckled together, the enraged Leopold leaped forward and with a mighty swipe of his paw sent Dandy sprawling across the den. "What are you laughing at?" he snarled. "Tear an arm from this man and bring it to me."

An involuntary hum leaked from Dandy's throat as he nodded and crept toward the man. Leopold was in no mood not to be taken seriously. But he discovered, to his surprise, that the man was now smiling—another thing the lions had never seen an evening meal do; he was kneeling with his uplifted face bathed in the light and his arms lifted toward the place where the light came from.

Something else was odd: No matter how hard Dandy tried, he could not break into that patch of brightness. Every time the tip of his nose touched the light, he quickly lost the ability to move. Then he noticed that one of the man's hands had lowered slightly and was sticking out of the shaft of light. This was an opportunity. Dandy curled his lips into a snarl and lunged. He could take hold of the arm with his teeth and drag the man out of the light—and the lions would finally be able to enjoy a gourmet dinner. Dandy might even be hailed as a hero.

What happened next haunted Dandy for the rest of his life. He lunged forward with a roar—and started licking the man's hand. When Dandy's rough tongue touched the man's hand, the man jerked it back so fast that he fell over backward. Dandy was mortified. His friend Tawny thought this was the funniest thing she had ever seen. "If you can't eat 'em, lick 'em," she roared as she rolled over on her back. Dandy sulked. He was hungry, but he was beginning to wonder if this particular meal was worth the trouble.

He looked over his shoulder, expecting Leopold to tear him to pieces for his failure. But Leopold had other problems—he was still drooling like an idiot. What was going on here? Many of Dandy's friends were milling around just outside the circle of light. Every few minutes a lion would try to attack the man. They would take great running, snarling leaps. As long as they were still within the den's gloom, the lions had that fierce, hungry look that terrifies all other animals. But once they reached the light, they would slink away in fear or suddenly lose interest.

Perhaps the man's smell would provide a clue to what was happening, thought Dandy. Maybe he was poisonous. Dandy had just stretched his neck out for a good sniff when the man began to do something else meals never did: He began to sing.

The lions fell all over each other as they scrambled back, trying to get away from the strange sound. Dandy had never heard singing before, only screaming. The entire pride shrank back. Some of the lions had pressed nervously against the walls. Others had fled to the inner passages and now peered from the darkness in fear and wonder. The man was standing now, with his arms still thrust high above him, and he was singing at the top of his lungs. And he still looked delicious. The "king of beasts" stood and watched a singing happy meal, and not a one dared to take a bite.

Leopold didn't much care for music. He'd had enough. He pinned Dandy against the wall and growled, "Kill him, or I'll kill *you*."

"Kill him yourself," Dandy heard himself saying, surprised at his own foolish courage. He had never stood up to Leopold before. For a brief second, Leopold looked at him as though he were deciding where to sink his fangs. Then he turned and walked toward the back of the cave, growling orders for everyone to follow him. In the darkest corner of the den, the lions huddled and argued over what strange power could be keeping them from enjoying the meal that stood there singing before them. There was plenty of growling—some of it was coming from empty stomachs, some of it from the frustration of not being able to fill them.

Finally Raja, the oldest and wisest of the lions, spoke. He pointed out that each lion who tried to destroy the man lost his or her power at the point of entering the ray of light. The light, Raja argued, must be what was protecting the man. There were low growls of agreement. The lions moved closer together and lowered their voices—although it is very hard for a lion to whisper. Amidst sinister rumbles, a plan began to form. In a few hours, the special night-light would vanish, as it always did, and with it would go the strange power that protected the man. When the light disappeared, the entire pride would dine in style. Just the thought of it caused Leopold to begin slobbering again.

The lions lay down to wait. Dandy maneuvered into position so that he would get the first chance to grab the man's leg. Time seemed to slow to a crawl. As Dandy lay there he wondered why the special light had not moved. One by one, the lions dozed off, and the cave became filled with soft sounds: lion snores, rumbling stomachs, an occasional whisper, and the speaking of the man, who seemed to be talking to someone in the sky above him, where the light was coming from; maybe he was talking to the light. It still hadn't moved when Dandy finally closed his eyes.

He was startled from a deep sleep by Tawny's cry. Her neck was stretched upward and her eyes were wide with fear. Soon all the lions were awake, and their eyes followed her gaze. Leopold gasped, and soon the den was filled with gasping. High up in the cave, sitting in a crevice, was a beautiful creature of light. From this creature there shone a wonderful light that streaked down and bathed the man in a protective glow even more radiant than the light of the sun. The lions couldn't take their eyes from the stunning creature.

A soft sense of peace filled the den, and suddenly, amazingly, no one was hungry anymore. Dandy looked around and was surprised to see all his friends lying down; many had gone back to sleep. Then he saw the most amazing sight of all. Leopold and Boris had moved into the circle of light and were lying down right beside the man. Dandy could only stand gaping in disbelief as the man smiled and sat down by the lions. His lips moved in a silent prayer as he reached out and stroked Leopold's mane. The man's hand was still buried in the coarse hair when he too fell asleep.

That's the way the king's guards found them in the morning.

At the first light of dawn, the king got up and hurried to the lions' den. When he came near the den, he called to Daniel in an anguished voice, "Daniel, servant of the living God, has

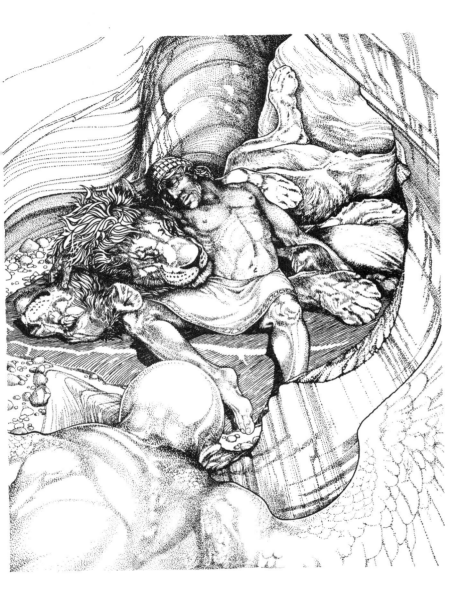

Leopold and Boris had moved into the circle of light
and were lying down right beside the man.

your God, whom you serve continually, been able to rescue you from the lions?"

Daniel answered, "O king, live forever! My God sent his angel, and he shut the mouths of the lions. They have not hurt me, because I was found innocent in his sight. Nor have I ever done any wrong before you, O king."

The king was overjoyed and gave orders to lift Daniel out of the den. And when Daniel was lifted from the den, no wound was found on him, because he had trusted in his God.

At the king's command, the men who had falsely accused Daniel were brought in and thrown into the lions' den, along with their wives and children. And before they reached the floor of the den, the lions overpowered them and crushed all their bones.

Then King Darius wrote to all the peoples, nations and men of every language throughout the land:

"May you prosper greatly!

"I issue a decree that in every part of my kingdom people must fear and reverence the God of Daniel.

"For he is the living God
and he endures forever;
his kingdom will not be destroyed,
his dominion will never end.
He rescues and he saves;
he performs signs and wonders
in the heavens and on the earth.
He has rescued Daniel
from the power of the lions."

So Daniel prospered during the reign of Darius and the reign of Cyrus the Persian.[2]

• • •

"A lion named Dandy," chortled Edgar. "Very funny."

It was rare to hear Edgar laugh at all, but the more he thought about it the more amused he became. "Dandy Lion. Sure, I get it, like the flower," he cackled.

Edgar's wings hung limply and tears rolled from his clouded eyes as he laughed. At any other time Galya would have been happy to see his friend laugh. But it seemed as though the raven had missed the whole point of the story. Galya had purposely chosen this story to show that God did *not* lack power, that He even had the power to seal the jaws of a mighty lion.

Yet Edgar had chosen to focus on a trivial detail rather than on the real truth. *Maybe I'm wasting my time,* Galya thought, as Edgar tried to recover. *Maybe Edgar's heart is so hardened that nothing can break through.* Galya couldn't tell if Edgar had heard anything other than Dandy's name. All he knew was that Edgar was enjoying himself immensely, and motioning for him to tell another story. Galya began with a passage he remembered from the Great Book.

The Sheepish Prophet

During that long period, the king of Egypt died. The Israelites groaned in their slavery and cried out, and their cry for help because of their slavery went up to God. God heard their groaning and he remembered his covenant with Abraham, with Isaac and with Jacob. So God looked on the Israelites and was concerned about them.

Now Moses was tending the flock of Jethro his father-in-law, the priest of Midian, and he led the flock to the far side of the desert and came to Horeb, the mountain of God. There the angel of the LORD appeared to him in flames of fire from within a bush.[1]

The Burning Bush

It was a fine day and a rare patch of grass, and the sheep was enjoying both of them. He was nibbling the juicy blades when a great commotion broke the afternoon quiet.

The sheep looked up just in time to see Herman coming. It's rare to see a sheep galloping; they're much better at skipping along. But Herman was slung low to the

Herman was the quiet type—not really the sort of sheep they
expected to catch on fire. But there he was, slumped in
the water, smelling like a smoky, wet mitten.

ground, a dirty white blur leading a trail of white smoke. The other sheep parted immediately, giving Herman a wide berth.

In this part of the world, burning sheep have the right of way. And there was no mistake about it—Herman was on fire and more than eager to reach the water hole. He hit the shallow pool at full speed, plunked his rump into the water with a sizzle and a splash, and let out a long, slow sigh of relief.

The other sheep eyed each other curiously. Herman was the quiet type—not really the sort of sheep they expected to catch on fire. But there he was, slumped in the water, smelling like a smoky, wet mitten. No one likes to be set on fire, but for sheep the idea is a particularly unpleasant one. Unless the fire is put out immediately, it'll find its way into the wool and smolder for a long time.

For this reason, sheep are very good about heeding the dangers of campfires. They often tell their children the legend of Mutton—a story passed down for generations of sheep, and one guaranteed to make a young lamb steer clear of fires.

One cool evening, the story went, a careless sheep named Mutton got his feet tangled beneath him and stumbled into a campfire. Mutton reacted as any animal might, trying to run in several directions at once. After a frantic chase, the shepherds finally managed to tackle the bleating sheep and wrestle him to the ground. They threw dirt and blankets on him, assuming they had stifled the flames. But where wool is concerned, fire can be quiet and sneaky. Mutton's coat smoldered for several days without anyone realizing it.

Then one night, while Mutton was sleeping, he burst back into flame. The rest of the story is too unpleasant to share, but it was enough to give any sheep a healthy respect for fire safety. To this day, the name *Mutton* is known for the tragic combination of sheep and fire.

And now, the exact same thing had happened to Herman. All he could do was hunker down in the water hole, shake his head, and bleat out the story of how he came to have a burning rump. When at last he stood to inspect the damage, one final wisp of smoke drifted up from his backside. The entire flock crowded around Herman with his singed wet wool, eager to hear his story.

Herman had been minding his own business, enjoying an after-noon snack of weeds beneath a desert shrub when the shrub burst into flames without warning. There was no alarm, no whiff of smoke—just fire from nowhere. Where was that sudden heat com-ing from? Herman turned to find out what was burning, not real-izing that he was part of the answer.

It was a strange fire that danced before his eyes—a fire from a bush. The heat was intense, but there was no smell of smoke and the bush didn't burn up—no ashes, no smoke, and not even the usual crackle of a fire. Herman wondered what the shepherd would think about all this. Then he saw that the man was already staring at the curious flame, and Herman stepped aside as the shepherd walked up to examine the bush.

> Moses saw that though the bush was on fire it did not burn up. So Moses thought, "I will go over and see this strange sight—why the bush does not burn up."
>
> When the LORD saw that he had gone over to look, God called to him from within the bush, "Moses! Moses!"
>
> And Moses said, "Here I am."[2]

Herman almost jumped out of his fleece. He could handle a little spontaneous combustion, but a talking bush was another thing. He hit the ground running. About fifty yards away, he stopped and looked back. His heart was racing. In his short life, Herman had heard the dry, sinister whisper of a snake; he had shivered as coyotes barked hunting instructions at the first light of dawn; he had heard spooky owls hooting their greetings to each other on a moonlit night. But he had *never* heard a bush speak. It scared him to death! If a *burn-ing* bush doesn't get your attention, a *talking* bush will certainly do the trick.

The bush spoke directly to the shepherd; it called him Moses. Until that moment, Herman had never heard the shepherd's name. But the bush spoke his name with such authority that the ground trembled.

The voice was frightening, but there was also something won-derful about it—something that quieted Herman's racing heart and

drew
him back
toward the bush.
As he turned and
made his way back, lis-
tening carefully to the
voice, he still didn't realize there were embers
smoldering in his wool.

Herman stood, almost
in a trance, as the rest of
the frightened flock watched
from a distant hill. This was
the voice of the Creator—
the One called God! In the
quiet of the night, as a full
moon set the earth aglow and
stars adorned the sky like diamonds, Herman had heard the shepherd whisper the name of God. Just the sound of His name had filled
him with hope and peace.

Now, standing in the sunlight and hearing the Holy One speak
made Herman feel beautiful, part of something so much bigger than
his own little world. How honored the shepherd must be that God
would speak directly to him, that He would call him by name.

The shepherd was affected by the voice, too. As soon as he knew
who was speaking, his curiosity turned to fear and reverence. Herman
waited, frozen with awe, watching to see what would happen next.

"Do not come any closer," God said. "Take off your san-
dals, for the place where you are standing is holy ground." Then

he said, "I am the God of your father, the God of Abraham, the God of Isaac and the God of Jacob." At this, Moses hid his face, because he was afraid to look at God.

The LORD said, "I have indeed seen the misery of my people in Egypt. I have heard them crying out because of their slave drivers, and I am concerned about their suffering. So I have come down to rescue them from the hand of the Egyptians and to bring them up out of that land into a good and spacious land, a land flowing with milk and honey—the home of the Canaanites, Hittites, Amorites, Perizzites, Hivites and Jebusites. And now the cry of the Israelites has reached me, and I have seen the way the Egyptians are oppressing them. So now, go. I am sending you to Pharaoh to bring my people the Israelites out of Egypt."[3]

Herman's heart raced. He had seen firsthand the cruelty of the Egyptians, who were the brutal masters of Moses' people, their slaves. Once Herman had seen a man beaten to death. The man was very sick; he could no longer support one of the harnesses men had to use to pull huge blocks of stone. There were nearly one hundred men pulling together, and the sick one kept falling to the ground. The last time he fell, several of the other workers stumbled over his frail body. They tried to help him to his feet, but the Egyptian in charge had pushed them back. Cursing with rage, he had whipped the man, then kicked him until he was no longer moving.

Herman had felt nauseated for days after seeing such cruelty. The slaves and shepherds whispered frightening stories of friends who had been executed at the slightest whim of the Egyptians. Little children died trying to perform labor that would have tested the strength of an adult.

All these things saddened Herman, but now there was hope. Moses, Herman's very own shepherd, was being sent by the Creator to lead God's children out of horror and into hope. What an honor for him to be chosen! What an honor to be a sheep with the chance to witness such an event. Herman inched forward, his chin a little higher and his step a little prouder.

Neighborhood Party

Date: Saturday, August 2, 2003

Time: 6:00

Sandra - Aug / 1st
Sandra

4330 & 4310 Fallen Leaf Lane

Melody Ranch

Please bring your
favorite Hors d'oeurve
and beer or wine
Kid's cuisine provided

Kindly reply:
Kathe & Bill Coelho
739-2340
Kim & Lew Parker
739-8766

We hope you can come and
join the fun!

A Reluctant Hero

> But Moses said to God, "Who am I, that I should go to Pharaoh and bring the Israelites out of Egypt?"[4]

A bleat escaped from Herman's throat. He was incredulous. *Who am I?* What kind of answer was that? This was the God of the universe speaking—and using a burning bush, for pity sake! What kind of a man would ask, "Who am I?"

If only I could speak, Herman thought. *I would scold this shy shepherd. I would show him how foolish it is to hesitate when God calls.*

Herman was just a lowly sheep. He knew his was not the most respected role in creation. But if God were to speak *his* name, he knew he would not hesitate. His ancestors had been selected as sacrifices to this God for many generations. Winegart, Beldone, Guesteau—these were all names of honor among sheep, known among every flock because of their sacrifices. They had given all they had to give—their very lives. When the time came, sheep could be as courageous as any animal.

But the Creator was not asking Moses for his life, merely his service—his obedience. And Moses had answered, "Who am I?"

"I'll tell you who you are!" Herman wanted to shout. "You're the one He chose! He considers you equal to the task. Stop acting like a frightened little lamb. *Go!*"

But sheep can't speak, at least not in a way humans can understand. So Herman just shifted his weight from hoof to hoof and made unhappy little bleating sounds. Moses heard Herman and turned in his direction, but at that very moment, the voice spoke again.

> And God said, "I will be with you. And this will be the sign to you that it is I who have sent you: When you have brought the people out of Egypt, you will worship God on this mountain."
>
> Moses said to God, "Suppose I go to the Israelites and say to them, 'The God of your fathers has sent me to you,' and they ask me, 'What is his name?' Then what shall I tell them?"

God said to Moses, "I AM WHO I AM. This is what you are
to say to the Israelites: 'I AM has sent me to you.'"[5]

There could be no doubting it now. This was the one true God.
Herman looked at Moses, who was now standing quietly, looking
as though he had just been told he had hoof-and-mouth disease. The
bush continued to burn silently.

A deep sadness washed over Herman. Just across the desert, thousands of men, women, and children—loved ones of this majestic Creator—were dying. Many of those still alive longed for the rest that
only death could bring. Their salvation was near! Yet, here, slouch-
ing in the midst of a miracle, in the presence of the One who made
the world, was a man who could make a difference, but made excuses
instead! "I'm not the right man . . . I'm not much of a speaker. . .
I'll probably only mess up. . . I'd like to, really, but . . ."

Herman wondered for a moment if a good swift sheep kick in
the rear might snap Moses out of his pity party. How he wished he
could speak. The flame from the bush flared up with a roar. Herman
realized that if a strange burning, talking bush could not get through
to Moses, a nagging sheep most likely wouldn't do any better. The
Creator had promised to go with Moses; He even promised to give
Moses the words he needed in order to do the job. But the shepherd only stood there, shrugging his shoulders in helplessness.

Herman shook his head in frustration and thought about making his way back toward the flock. But then the earth beneath him
began to shake. The great voice spoke again, and Herman pricked
up his ears to listen.

"Say to the Israelites, 'The LORD, the God of your fathers—
the God of Abraham, the God of Isaac and the God of Jacob—
has sent me to you.' This is my name forever, the name by which
I am to be remembered from generation to generation.

"Go, assemble the elders of Israel and say to them, 'The
LORD, the God of your fathers—the God of Abraham, Isaac
and Jacob—appeared to me and said: I have watched over
you and have seen what has been done to you in Egypt. And

I have promised to bring you up out of your misery in Egypt into the land of the Canaanites, Hittites, Amorites, Perizzites, Hivites and Jebusites—a land flowing with milk and honey.'

"The elders of Israel will listen to you. Then you and the elders are to go to the king of Egypt and say to him, 'The LORD, the God of the Hebrews, has met with us. Let us take a three-day journey into the desert to offer sacrifices to the LORD our God.' But I know that the king of Egypt will not let you go unless a mighty hand compels him. So I will stretch out my hand and strike the Egyptians with all the wonders that I will perform among them. After that, he will let you go.

"And I will make the Egyptians favorably disposed toward this people, so that when you leave you will not go empty-handed. Every woman is to ask her neighbor and any woman living in her house for articles of silver and gold and for clothing, which you will put on your sons and daughters. And so you will plunder the Egyptians."[6]

There it was. What more could Moses need? What more assurance could he want? Surely he would respond now, for God had given just the words to light another fire—under Moses. Herman looked at him eagerly, seeking the glimmer of excitement that ought to be shining from the shepherd's eyes. But all he saw was more doubt and fear.

Moses answered, "What if they do not believe me or listen to me and say, 'The LORD did not appear to you'?"[7]

This time Herman ignored Moses. He spoke directly to the bush. "*I* believe you!" he bleated. "I'll go! Over here—yes, me, the sheep! Please send *me!*"

Herman figured any bush that had the ability to speak Hebrew could understand the language of sheep. The bush must have heard and understood, but Herman knew deep down that this was a thing about men and women, not about sheep—and God had already made His choice. He had chosen the best, but the best was not giving his best response.

This time Herman ignored Moses. He spoke directly to the bush. "*I* believe you!" bleated. "I'll go! Over here—yes, me, the sheep! Please send *me!*"

Herman wondered what kind of self-doubt and fear could cause someone to be so lukewarm about such an exciting adventure. Moses, of all men, had been chosen to become a great champion for his own people. He was born for this purpose. He had been invited to be God's partner in a fabulous expedition. He had even been given a promise of victory, and still he stood in silence.

Was God going to have to set the whole desert on fire? At least Moses could have come up with an original excuse. "What if they stake me to a pile of fire ants?" might at least have been an interesting objection. "What if they slice me to pieces with their swords?" That would have been a fair question. But all Moses could come up with was, "What if they don't believe me?"

> Then the LORD said to him, "What is that in your hand?"
> "A staff," he replied.
> The LORD said, "Throw it on the ground."
> Moses threw it on the ground and it became a snake, and he ran from it. Then the LORD said to him, "Reach out your hand and take it by the tail." So Moses reached out and took hold of the snake and it turned back into a staff in his hand. "This," said the LORD, "is so that they may believe that the LORD, the God of their fathers—the God of Abraham, the God of Isaac and the God of Jacob—has appeared to you."
>
> Then the LORD said, "Put your hand inside your cloak." So Moses put his hand into his cloak, and when he took it out, it was leprous, like snow.
>
> "Now put it back into your cloak," he said. So Moses put his hand back into his cloak, and when he took it out, it was restored, like the rest of his flesh.
>
> Then the LORD said, "If they do not believe you or pay attention to the first miraculous sign, they may believe the second. But if they do not believe these two signs or listen to you, take some water from the Nile and pour it on the dry ground. The water you take from the river will become blood on the ground."[8]

As Herman told the whole story to the wide-eyed sheep audience by the water hole, he said, "I wish you could have seen Moses

when that staff turned into a snake! One minute he held this beau-
tifully carved staff in his hand, and the next minute it lay hissing at
his feet. This was no harmless garden snake either—I'm talking about
a nasty, aggressive, 'if it bites you, you die' kind of snake!" Herman
hissed the word "sssssnake" for
effect, and then paused to enjoy the
frightened gasps of his audience.

"The second that snake
appeared," said Herman, "it coiled
to strike—not fast enough to get
the better of Moses, however. At
the first hiss, Moses lifted his gar-
ment, put his knees to the breeze,
and bolted! He was hurdling cac-
tus plants and clumps of brush like a deer. The voice from the bush
had to call twice to get him to come back." At this, some of the sheep
laughed—a good chuckle was a welcome relief after that snake part.

After that, as Herman informed his rapt audience, God commanded
the shepherd to pick up the snake. Moses circled the snake three times,
but each time he reached for the snake, it would strike at him. He
looked toward the bush. "Take it by the tail," the bush commanded.

Keeping his body as far from the snake as possible, Moses finally
stretched out his arm and seized the snake by the tail. With the touch
of his hand, the snake began to stiffen and become transformed into
a staff again! Herman blinked and took another look to be sure his
eyes weren't deceiving him. It was the most amazing thing he'd ever
witnessed. At this point, Herman had remembered that the other
sheep had been watching from a safe distance, and he turned to
call them to come take a look for themselves. But the rest of the
sheep were long gone. Bushes and flames, maybe—but snakes were
too much. They had fled in fright.

"Well," thought Herman, "this snake bit is sure to convince him."
Now Moses would *have* to get excited about God's assignment. With
this kind of power, the shepherd didn't have to persuade those Egyptians; God would do the convincing. One look at the "instant snake"
trick, and the pharaoh would surely let Moses' people go.

"Take it by the tail," the bush commanded. Keeping his body as far from the snake as possible, Moses finally stretched out his arm and seized the snake by the tail. With the touch of his hand, the snake began to stiffen and become transformed into a staff again!

Moses said to the LORD, "O Lord, I have never been eloquent, neither in the past nor since you have spoken to your servant. I am slow of speech and tongue."[9]

Herman started bleating in disdain and couldn't stop. Never had he felt such frustration. God's sole choice for leading the people to freedom was a hopeless coward! Herman was willing to step in and help, but he was unable to communicate. Would there ever be anyone willing to make the necessary sacrifice in order to save God's people?

Abruptly Herman stopped bleating and his eyes grew wide. He smelled smoke. It wasn't the smell of a burning bush; it was the smell of burning wool! He looked around and saw smoke curling from his backside. At that same instant, the fire reached his skin. He took off like a flaming arrow shot from a bow.

As he crested the hill at the spot where his friends had disappeared, Herman heard the roar of flames and the voice of God, but he couldn't hear what the voice said. He could see the flock and, just beyond them, an oasis. They wasted no time getting out of his way.

But Moses said, "O Lord, please send someone else to do it."

Then the LORD's anger burned against Moses and he said, "What about your brother, Aaron the Levite? I know he can speak well. He is already on his way to meet you, and his heart will be glad when he sees you. You shall speak to him and put words in his mouth; I will help both of you speak and will teach you what to do. He will speak to the people for you, and it will be as if he were your mouth and as if you were God to him. But take this staff in your hand so you can perform miraculous signs with it."

Then Moses went back to Jethro his father-in-law and said to him, "Let me go back to my own people in Egypt to see if any of them are still alive."

Jethro said, "Go, and I wish you well."

Now the LORD had said to Moses in Midian, "Go back to Egypt, for all the men who wanted to kill you are dead." So Moses took his wife and sons, put them on a donkey and started back to Egypt. And he took the staff of God in his hand.[10]

● ● ●

"So what's the point of *this* story?" squawked Edgar. "Sheeesh! First you tell me a story of Paradise ruined, and you make out the villain to be a character like me. *Then* you slay me with Dandy Lion."

An involuntary chuckle escaped from Edgar's throat. "And now you come up with this tale of a sheepish leader—no offense intended. We ravens don't have many stories, but the few we do tell have happy endings."

"I really don't know, Edgar, what you might see as the point of this one," Galya replied. "My mother used to love telling me about Herman, and at the ending she would always say that it all goes to show that God can use *anybody*—even, as you put it, 'a sheepish leader.' God wasn't looking for a ready-made hero. He was looking for an ordinary fellow willing to trust an extraordinary God." After a long pause he added, "Maybe He can use me."

Galya had become thoughtful. He now seemed to be talking to himself as much as Edgar. "There's something woven carefully into all these stories," he said. "It's something that has fanned the flame of hope within me. I'm always struck by the notion in these tales that God cares enough to pay attention to us. Why did He put up with Adam? Why did He keep going after Moses when He could have moved on to someone else? For that matter, why didn't He just discard this world, as tangled up and confused as it had become, and start over?"

Galya paused. He opened his mouth to begin telling Edgar the story of the flood, in which God had done just that. Then, on second thought, he changed his mind, because Edgar had begun to speak.

"You expect me to have an answer?" scoffed Edgar. "There are no answers. It's all poppycock to me! If you ask me, you God-lovers choose some very strange heroes: an elephant who can't keep his feet under him; humans who can't follow orders; a leader with a confidence problem; and finally, a God who can't control His own creation! You're a fool, Galya. If God is so good, how come your stories are so bad? How come my moth—"

Edgar let the final syllable die in his throat. It was the word he never said out loud, and the question he never dared to ask. He didn't even dare to let his mind and heart go there.

"But the story doesn't end there," Galya sputtered. "God kept His promise! He *did* use Moses to free the people, and Herman lived to see it happen."

Galya paused, sure that Edgar was going to throw in some nasty comment or say that he'd had enough of these stories. But Edgar had suddenly grown quiet and was staring off into the distance.

So Galya began to tell him the story of how God *did* use Moses to rescue the people. He told him the story of Clarence.

Clarence

The Longing

The military column filed by with pomp and pageantry. Clarence watched it all, and he burned with envy.

It had been just another day of relentless work when the Egyptian army had suddenly appeared in a proud procession. Clarence was astounded by the elegance of the steeds pulling the ornately appointed chariots. What beautiful and impressive horses they were!

These stallions didn't plod along, snorting, with heads hung low. Instead they marched in perfect step, lifting their hoofs high in the air, pausing momentarily, then clapping them to the earth with neat precision. The pause at the peak of each step created the illusion of the warriors floating in midair, pulling the chariot effortlessly behind them. As each horse passed, muscles rippling, necks regally arched, and nostrils flaring, they stared straight ahead, as though nothing else was worthy of their glance.

Clarence sighed. This was the way he had always seen himself in daydreams. This was what horses were born to be. This was the kind of life he dreamed about every night.

This was what horses were born to be.

An involuntary whinny escaped Clarence's throat, and he lowered his head. He shuddered in shame and stared down at the earth beneath his feet. Here he stood, in the presence of all this magnificence and might—Clarence, covered with mud, his mane matted and ropy, his life spent toiling away in the mire of mediocrity.

The rickety cart Clarence pulled didn't blaze with color. It had no gold inlay like those dazzling Egyptian chariots. It didn't carry a regal soldier or a noble lord. No, his cart was filled with the dirt of excavation, the dregs of "progress." His cart contained the sweat and blood of human suffering, the muck of misery.

No prince or general held Clarence's reins. An insignificant slave held the filthy rope that circled his neck. Clarence shook his head and snorted. No matter how much he dreamed of being a part of the glory passing before him, no matter how confident he was that he could pull a majestic chariot, he'd never made it any farther than the humiliating task of moving Egyptian dirt.

His situation was all the more painful because he had the same bloodline as the horses that pranced so nobly by him now. Clarence was powerfully built and gifted with incredible speed. There had been a day when several of the Egyptian horses had escaped from their pasture and trotted by the fields where Clarence was kept. They mocked the humble stables of the working horses; they boasted of their own rich and royal surroundings. These military stallions were amazed that none of the horses that labored for the Israelites had ever tasted the fine grain they enjoyed each day. They laughed and snorted at the sparse weeds that served as dinner for Clarence and his friends.

One day the Egyptian stallions challenged Clarence and his workmates to a race. The clear purpose was to show how fast the well-fed, well-trained royal horses were. But when the vast line of horses broke into a wild gallop, a great surprise was in store. It wasn't one of the royal stallions who surged to the front—it was Clarence. The Egyptian steeds were furious, and they challenged him to a rematch.

The results were the same: Clarence was the fastest of the pack, though it didn't help his popularity. The Egyptian stallions made fun of him and treated him as something far beneath their proud stature—at least all but one of them treated him this way. The exception was a beautiful black mare with the name of Zebell. She was different from the others. One day she spoke to Clarence when none of the others were around. "Why don't you come away and join us?" she asked.

Clarence simply tossed his head away shyly. To say the least, he was surprised by the invitation. He could well imagine the ridicule he would suffer if he were ever bold enough to try such a thing. But Zebell was persistent. "You're a fine figure of a horse, though you don't even realize it," she smiled. "You deserve much better than the life of labor you struggle through. Now, listen carefully." Zebell drew close, checking vigilantly to be sure no one was listening. Clarence could see her eyes flashing with excitement and mischief.

"If you trotted back to the royal stables with our group," said Zebell, "I'm certain you could blend right in. You're as fine as we are, and who would notice one extra horse? And once inside our camp, your speed and strength would lift you to a position of pride. Some fine soldier would be certain to claim you—or perhaps even a lord from Pharaoh's palace!"

Zebell's soothing voice made Clarence's heart beat even faster than the race had done. Wasn't this, after all, the kind of opportunity he had longed for all his life? Wasn't this the answer to his prayers?

Clarence believed that God loved the people of Israel and that He had plans for them. But Clarence was tired of suffering meekly in the shadow of the magnificent wealth and power of Egypt. He was tired of foraging for scrubby tufts of grass. He was ashamed of being associated with people who might never be anything more than slaves.

Clarence dreamed of strutting his stuff in the corridors of power. He could see himself glittering with the silver and gold that adorned Pharaoh's horses, flexing his muscles and proving his speed before people who lived in palaces. Now he was being offered that prospect.

The black mare nuzzled him gently, massaging him with compliments and praise. Clarence needed no further encouragement.

This was clearly the opportunity of a lifetime. He would accompany Pharaoh's horses, the beautiful Zebell at his side. Was it a risk? Perhaps, but the potential reward made it a risk worth taking. This was Clarence's big chance.

But the chance was snatched away as fast as it was offered. At that very moment a group of Egyptian soldiers appeared over the crest of a nearby hill. Onward they came, shouting and waving swords at their runaway stable of stallions. Slapping the horses with the flat side of their swords, they quickly separated Pharaoh's steeds from those of the Israelites and began herding them back to camp. And that was that!

Clarence wasn't ready to give in just yet. He tried to follow the pack, but the soldiers caught sight of him every time. "Here now! Get away!" they'd yell, accentuating their words with flicks of their whips. Maybe if he joined the black mare, her acceptance would persuade the soldiers to let him stay. He whinnied, then galloped toward her, but she seemed afraid to acknowledge him. He tried it three times with no luck. Then, frustrated, he charged directly into the center of the group.

The sting of a whip brought him up short. Clarence heard a curse, and, from the corner of his eye, he saw one of the soldiers pull an arrow from his quiver. That was enough to break his spirit. Clarence charged away at a sprint, dashing quickly out of range.

His opportunity for greatness had been so close, but now it was over. As the Egyptian horses rumbled to the top of the hill, the black mare stopped. Silhouetted against the sky, she turned and reared up, her front legs flailing the air. The sound of her voice tore at his heart. Then she wheeled and disappeared over the hill.

And in that moment, Clarence vowed that somehow he would escape. He would join the Egyptians—he was determined—and they would accept him into their circles of power and luxury.

The clanging of armor brought him back to the present moment. Clarence was watching in shame as the great military procession filed by. The chariots had passed, and now the soldiers were riding in a single column that stretched back as far as Clarence could see. How majestic they looked in their shining armor and headgear.

The crowds by the roadside stepped back several paces as the soldiers passed. The horses were draped with beautiful blankets, and they wore ornately decorated saddles that creaked with every step.

The smell of saddle oil, steel, and leather mingled in an intoxicating aroma that once again stirred Clarence's resolve. The love of his family and the faith of the Israelites faded in importance. His sense of purpose, his knowledge of rightness, and his awareness of God faded in the dazzle of the silver and gold before him. Someday his talents would no longer be wasted on slaves and downtrodden people. Clarence would find the fame he deserved. It must happen!

Clarence looked for Zebell in the procession, but she was nowhere to be seen. Finally the last soldier rode by, and only the soldiers' dust remained in the road. Clarence returned sadly to the drab reality of his life.

The days that followed were filled with confusion and doubt. There were whispers that Moses, the leader of the Israelites, had boldly demanded that Pharaoh release the people of Israel. And Pharaoh, naturally enough, only scoffed. Why should he free the people who provided useful slave labor?

But stranger things than this bold request were happening— strange things called plagues. One day, as Clarence went about his work down by the great river Nile, he heard cries of bewilderment and panic. The screaming grew louder and louder until it echoed all around the banks where Clarence stood. Two scrawny nags brought the news.

> All the water was changed into blood. The fish in the Nile died, and the river smelled so bad that the Egyptians could not drink its water. Blood was everywhere in Egypt. . . .
>
> And all the Egyptians dug along the Nile to get drinking water, because they could not drink the water of the river.[1]

Rivers of blood! It was an unthinkable notion, and fear and confusion spread like a disease. The Egyptians were announcing that new water had to be found immediately. So Clarence, his animal friends, and thousands of Israelites were pressed into duty helping to dig new wells. Yet when he returned to the place of the Israelites, he was surprised to discover there was plenty of water there. Only the Egyptians had been struck by the crisis.

On another day, as Clarence was clearing stumps, he heard an ominous hum. The sky grew dark, and the persistence of the noise made Clarence think he might go mad. What could be causing it? As he labored to pull his cart, millions of gnats converged on the scene—so many that they blocked out the sun.

●   ●   ●

"A gnat banquet!" Edgar screeched. "Raven heaven! I could eat my fill just by gliding through the swarm with an open mouth."

Galya paused in his story and stared at the impudent black bird before him. Edgar seemed to hold no respect for anything or anyone. He lacked any empathy or compassion. Most of the time he simply stared into the distance and let Galya tell his stories. He did seem at times to be engrossed in the narrative, but then he'd interrupt with some banal comment like, "Gnat banquet!"

It seemed as though Edgar was trying to keep the message of the stories from getting through to him—as though he was using the shield of sarcasm to deflect the warmth and goodness of the stories so they wouldn't touch his heart or stir his soul.

"What?" pleaded Edgar with a mock innocence as he caught Galya's icy stare. "I thought you were interested in my point of view. Apparently not! Well—speak on, Little Lamb." He gestured impatiently with a wing, and settled back down to listen.

Galya continued.

●   ●   ●

One gnat is merely something to flick away with one's tail. Five or six are no big concern. But clouds of them! Millions! Clarence clamped his eyes shut and braced for the agony of gnats engulfing him and drinking his blood.

But not a single gnat landed on Clarence or any of his friends. The swarms of gnats caused no problem in the Israelite camp, unless you counted their maddening hum. It could be heard all day long, as millions of gnats flew right over them en route to Egyptian flesh. And the hum was united with the screams of those Egyptians.

But that was only one of the awful plagues. The stench of death was everywhere as, day after day, the Egyptians struggled with some new deadly disaster. Soldiers could be seen riding sickly horses—though once again, the working horses of the Israelites were spared. Many of those same soldiers suffered from open sores and boils.

It seemed like the plagues would never stop. One afternoon, the skies darkened and the worst storm Clarence had ever seen pounded the horizon. Then the air turned ice-cold.

> The LORD sent thunder and hail, and lightning flashed down to the ground. So the LORD rained hail on the land of Egypt; hail fell and lightning flashed back and forth. It was the worst storm in all the land of Egypt since it had become a nation. Throughout Egypt hail struck everything in the fields—both men and animals; it beat down everything growing in the fields and stripped every tree. The only place it did not hail was the land of Goshen, where the Israelites were.[2]

Plague after gruesome plague, the Israelite camp came out unscathed while their taskmasters were stricken by terrible disasters. There could be only one explanation: The Egyptians were being punished for their refusal to free the Israelite slaves. Who had the power to send the plagues but God Himself? And yet even now, even with this turn of events, Clarence felt a burning desire to be in those rich, luxurious stables and to march with a conquering army. For when all was said and done, he still lived with poor people. He was still a grimy, forgotten workhorse.

Perhaps there *would* be some punishment from heaven if Clarence were to break ranks with the Israelites and join their masters—but the reward would have to make the punishment worthwhile, wouldn't it? He could say his prayers of confession and apology while munching on the sweet hay of the royal stables.

Clarence also dreamed of Zebell—and often. Had she found shelter during the storms? Had she escaped the diseases and the terrible plagues? He dared not even entertain the thought that she might be among the casualties. Although he wanted no part of the dangers experienced by her group, he longed to be with her all the same.

But there were moments of doubt, too. Clarence saw the Israelites, kept safe and secure all through the chaos, and he had a nagging thought: *Perhaps the God of the Israelites is truly powerful. Perhaps He could bring down this nation of slave owners.*

Clarence thought of his own kind, poor but safe; he thought of their masters, rich but endangered. And he wasn't sure what to think or what to hope for. There was the greatness of the Egyptians—and the God of the Israelites. He felt pulled between the two. He knew the right thing to do, but he couldn't understand how the right thing held out any hope for him. Was there nothing more in life than to toil in the sun until he dropped? If he ran away, would he feel guilty for the rest of his life? It seemed that the ground trembled, no matter which way he turned.

Meanwhile, the Israelites were beginning to grumble. Some were willing to give their lives to be free from the tyranny and cruelty of the Egyptians, but others wondered what they would do and where they would go if they managed to break free—and worse yet, what if, having tasted freedom, they were caught and returned to bondage once again? Just like Clarence, the Israelites were pulled in two directions.

The time was coming when Clarence would have to make a choice. All he wanted was to be on the winning side. No! More than that, he wanted to be a winner himself—and to be recognized as one. What a joy it would be if just once he could celebrate his day in the light as the steed of a master rather than the nag of a slave.

That evening, as the bloodred sun hung low in the sky, a group of Egyptian soldiers rode along the horizon. Clarence's heart skipped a beat. The last soldier's mount hesitated and pranced in circles, reluctant to go where she was directed. The horse whinnied in desperation. Clarence recognized the voice immediately—it was Zebell! He galloped toward her eagerly, calling her name. But as quickly as she had appeared, she was gone. Clarence called out in desperation, but there was only silence.

These were days Clarence thought he could not survive.
Then a terrible night came. Clarence was awakened as the air
was pierced with the screams of Egyptian mothers and fathers.

> At midnight the LORD struck down all the firstborn in
> Egypt, from the firstborn of Pharaoh, who sat on the throne,
> to the firstborn of the prisoner, who was in the dungeon, and
> the firstborn of all the livestock as well. Pharaoh and all his offi-
> cials and all the Egyptians got up during the night, and there
> was loud wailing in Egypt, for there was not a house with-
> out someone dead.[3]

Clarence never heard exactly what had happened, but the mourn-
ful wails of tens of thousands of people kept him from sleeping that
night. It was said that this was the final and worst of all the plagues—
the disaster that changed everything. The lives of the Egyptians would
never be the same, and neither would those of the Israelites.

The very next day there were frantic movements and packing of possessions among the Israelites. The whole camp was on the move. The king of Egypt had agreed to let them go. Singing filled the air, and laughter soared on the wings of the wind.

But Clarence bowed his head. His chance for recognition and fame was gone forever.

ON THE RUN

The Egyptians urged the people to hurry and leave the country. "For otherwise," they said, "we will all die!" So the people took their dough before the yeast was added, and carried it on their shoulders in kneading troughs wrapped in clothing. The Israelites did as Moses instructed and asked the Egyptians for articles of silver and gold and for clothing. The LORD had made the Egyptians favorably disposed toward the people, and they gave them what they asked for; so they plundered the Egyptians.

The Israelites journeyed from Rameses to Succoth. There were about six hundred thousand men on foot, besides women and children. Many other people went up with them, as well as large droves of livestock, both flocks and herds. With the dough they had brought from Egypt, they baked cakes of unleavened bread. The dough was without yeast because they had been driven out of Egypt and did not have time to prepare food for themselves. . . .

After leaving Succoth they camped at Etham on the edge of the desert. By day the LORD went ahead of them in a pillar of cloud to guide them on their way and by night in a pillar of fire to give them light, so that they could travel by day or night. Neither the pillar of cloud by day nor the pillar of fire by night left its place in front of the people.

Then the LORD said to Moses, "Tell the Israelites to turn back and encamp near Pi Hahiroth, between Migdol and the sea. They are to encamp by the sea, directly opposite Baal Zephon. Pharaoh will think, 'The Israelites are wandering around the land in confusion, hemmed in by the desert.' And

I will harden Pharaoh's heart, and he will pursue them. But I will gain glory for myself through Pharaoh and all his army, and the Egyptians will know that I am the LORD." So the Israelites did this.

When the king of Egypt was told that the people had fled, Pharaoh and his officials changed their minds about them and said, "What have we done? We have let the Israelites go and have lost their services!" So he had his chariot made ready and took his army with him. He took six hundred of the best chariots, along with all the other chariots of Egypt, with officers over all of them. The LORD hardened the heart of Pharaoh king of Egypt, so that he pursued the Israelites, who were marching out boldly. The Egyptians—all Pharaoh's horses and chariots, horsemen and troops—pursued the Israelites and overtook them as they camped by the sea near Pi Hahiroth, opposite Baal Zephon.[4]

These were days of confusion for Clarence, along with wonder, sadness, and fear. His eyes had almost popped out of his head when he first saw the column of smoke that led the people away from Egypt. And no one seemed to sleep that first night as they gazed at the awesome column of fire that towered over their camp. There could be no denying that this was a great adventure.

Yet, in spite of the miraculous things happening around him, Clarence longed for the rhythm of the life he had known. The days of toil had been backbreaking, but at least he had known what to expect each day. Certain hours to work, certain hours to rest, certain hours to eat—not the finest of food, of course, but he never went hungry. And Clarence had always been sustained by a glimmer of hope that he might escape, that someone might notice him and invite him into the glory and pageantry of Egypt.

Now all that was gone. There was no more slavery, but there was no security either. It seemed that Clarence's people were without a country, without direction, without hope of any kind. For there had been a terrible development. Pharaoh, who had given the order for the slaves to be set free, had changed his mind. He had sent his army out in pursuit of the fleeing Israelites. Now the deadly army stood on one side of the Israelites, and the shores of the Red Sea on the other. They were hemmed in! The awesome pillar of smoke and fire had led them into a trap. Even the Israelites knew they had come to the end of the road.

As Pharaoh approached, the Israelites looked up, and there were the Egyptians, marching after them. They were terrified and cried out to the LORD. They said to Moses, "Was it because there were no graves in Egypt that you brought us to the desert to die? What have you done to us by bringing us out of Egypt? Didn't we say to you in Egypt, 'Leave us alone; let us serve the Egyptians'? It would have been better for us to serve the Egyptians than to die in the desert!"...

Then the LORD said to Moses, "Why are you crying out to me? Tell the Israelites to move on."[5]

As one, the mass of people began moving toward the sea. There was clearly no place to go, but Moses had commanded the entire nation to continue marching, right into the water. As the throng of people and animals began to push forward, a roar of thunder and a rush of wind came out of nowhere. Strong as Clarence was, he was nearly knocked to the ground. The angel who had been moving ahead of them, along with the huge pillar of cloud, soared overhead and retreated toward the rear of the procession.

The confusion was beyond belief. Shouts of mutiny, cries of faith, and screams of fear mingled into one deafening roar.

Clarence could take no more. It was now or never. He reared and lashed out with his hooves, knocking down the slave who was holding him. The load of silver and clothing on his back fell away as he ran toward the Egyptian army. Clarence broke into a wild gallop as he approached the rear of the throng. Just ahead stood the pillar of cloud and the mighty angel bearing a flaming sword. Clarence veered to one side and stood with his flanks heaving, trying to catch his breath.

On the Israelite side of the pillar of cloud, the sky was as light as day, but on the Egyptian side there was a foreboding darkness. Clarence could make out chariots and horsemen riding back and forth in frustration along the line that separated the darkness from the light. But not one soldier could find a way to penetrate the line.

Clarence ran along the same line, calling out for Zebell. He wanted more than ever to join the Egyptians, but there was something about the darkness that had struck a deep terror in his heart. He could not cross over.

Clarence turned and ran along the line in the other direction, still looking for an opening. He pulled up so abruptly that he almost fell to the ground. In front of Clarence stood the angel—a magnificent, fearsome creature whose eyes burned brighter than fire. The finest and most decorated of Egyptian pharaohs and soldiers could never compare to such a presence.

The angel pointed toward the sea. Terrified, Clarence ran back toward his people. He stood at the rear of the throng, trembling uncontrollably. All the desires of his heart had run headlong into something that shattered his soul with lightning bolts of doubt. In the presence of the glory of God, the glory of the Egyptians appeared to be nothing but the utter darkness of death. Was that hope that he had seen in the face of the angel of God? How could it be? It seemed as though hope was gone. To turn back meant certain death; to go forward meant the same. There was no way to get to the Egyptians. Clarence lowered his head and, with his heart still pounding, joined the masses of Israelites moving toward the sea.

It was then that he heard an amazing sound—the sound of confusion and anger suddenly exploded into a shout of joy and praise. What was causing the commotion? Clarence was bringing up the rear of the great throng, and he could not see. He mustered all his speed to scramble up a rocky hill to get a better view—and Clarence caught his breath. He could see it all—thousands of Israelites surg-

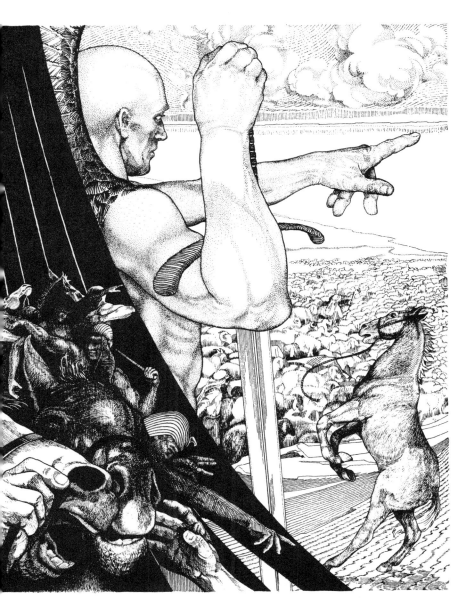

He pulled up so abruptly that he almost fell to the ground.
In front of Clarence stood the angel.

ing toward the Red Sea. About three-quarters of the way to the water's edge, Moses, Israel's leader, stood on an outcropping of rock. His arms were raised to the sky. A hot, rushing wind was sweeping over everyone. Then Clarence saw the miracle.

At the exact point where the Israelites had entered the water, there was a wide corridor of dry ground, stretching clear to the other side of the sea. On either side of the passage, the water boiled upward in a wall hundreds of feet high. Clarence stood frozen in utter amazement. The shouting had stopped. Hundreds of thousands of people and livestock moved toward the passageway in shocked silence. Who could speak? The rushing of the wind, the creaking of shifting loads atop the mules, and the shuffling of feet were the only sounds to be heard.

Clarence stumbled forward, his mind churning with questions. He was one of the last to enter. The ground was absolutely dry and solid. Inside the corridor, there was only the sound of the wind. Everyone moved forward without panic or fear. No horse or mule resisted; no baby cried; no one fell down or turned back.

Only once did Clarence glance over his shoulder, and once again terror struck his heart. The entire Egyptian army had charged into the corridor God had created through the sea.

> All that night the LORD drove the sea back with a strong east wind and turned it into dry land. The waters were divided, and the Israelites went through the sea on dry ground, with a wall of water on their right and on their left.
> The Egyptians pursued them, and all Pharaoh's horses and chariots and horsemen followed them into the sea.[6]

The hint of another day was just touching the horizon as Clarence, one of the last to make his way across, reached the other side. As he scrambled up the bank on the far side, he passed right by Moses. Clarence was curious to get a better look at the great leader.

Then he saw her at the front of the Egyptian throng—Zebell.

The black mare caught Clarence's eye and threw her head in the air, shaking it from side to side; her calls were smothered by the rushing of the wind. Clarence's heart quickened. Now was the time! No one could stop him now. This night he would join Zebell, and, once and for all, he would be on the winning side.

With a glance at Moses, Clarence reared and moved toward the sea. But then he hesitated. It was Moses, standing between Clarence and the sea, and there was something in his eyes. The great leader said nothing, but with his arms still raised and his staff still in his hand, he turned and gestured back toward the Egyptian army. Clarence's eyes widened in disbelief. Was the great leader going to allow him to pass?

As the last of the Israelites scrambled ashore, Clarence gingerly made his way down the embankment. When he reached the place where Moses was standing, he stopped once again. Zebell was closer, and now he could hear her calling out frantically. "Come away with us!" she screamed. "It's your last chance!"

Clarence looked at Moses, who once again sadly nodded in the direction of the Egyptians. Clarence followed his gaze. Behind Zebell, the Egyptians were erupting in a cauldron of confusion. He watched in amazement as the wheels fell from the chariots, and panicked horses threw their riders. Soldiers were staggering blindly as though they were lost. Many were cursing and fighting one another. God was dealing with the Egyptian attackers. This was what Moses wanted him to see. A wave of realization washed over Clarence. In the space of a split second, he saw the truth about himself, his people, and the rich life he had yearned to lead. Clarence was free to finally run to the Egyptians and to Zebell—but he would not do it.

It seemed so clear now: Clarence had been on the right side all along. He looked again at the throng of Israelites who had just crossed the sea. These were the children of a powerful God.

Clarence saw the Egyptians and their chariots for what they were. As for the Israelites, their rags no longer seemed ugly or shameful to him; they had a beauty all their own. There was a power among them that was so much greater than that of the Egyptian soldiers; there was strength so much greater than the legions of chariots. It had nothing to do with silver or gold; it was simply that these were God's children.

Clarence searched the crowd until he saw his master. The man he had knocked to the ground was whistling and gesturing wildly. Clarence wheeled and galloped back to an old master and a new life.

The day was beginning to dawn now, and a thunderous voice rolled from the heavens.

Then the LORD said to Moses, "Stretch out your hand over the sea so that the waters may flow back over the Egyptians and their chariots and horsemen." Moses stretched out his hand over the sea, and at daybreak the sea went back to its place. The Egyptians were fleeing toward it, and the LORD swept them into the sea. The water flowed back and covered the chariots and horsemen—the entire army of Pharaoh that had followed the Israelites into the sea. Not one of them survived.

But the Israelites went through the sea on dry ground, with a wall of water on their right and on their left. That day the LORD saved Israel from the hands of the Egyptians, and Israel saw the Egyptians lying dead on the shore. And when the Israelites saw the great power the LORD displayed against the Egyptians, the people feared the LORD and put their trust in him and in Moses his servant.[7]

Clarence worked hard for the rest of his life. He took pride in toiling for his master. He did find time, occasionally, to race the other stallions, or the wind itself. He found so much joy in the gifts God had given him, and he knew whom he should serve with these gifts. There were times of hardship and times of great joy. But for the rest of his long years, Clarence never forgot what he had seen that night, nor could he forget how close he had come to being deceived.

Clarence also never forgot the smile he saw on Moses' face when he chose to turn back and rejoin the people of Israel, the people of God—the true winners.

• • •

Edgar's Adventure

As Galya finished the story, Edgar seemed uncomfortable.

The troubled look in his eye was rare to see, and it never lasted long—which was the case this time as well.

"I'm gone," Edgar mumbled, as he hopped to the lowest rung of the fence. "Hungry, bored, and gone!"

With that, he flew off in a low, sweeping circle, testing the wind for food. Galya was tired as well. A skeptical listener makes for difficult storytelling. He could only be glad that Edgar had listened even this long; it was far more than he'd ever paid attention before. And Galya worried that soon there would be no more time for stories— that there would be no one to share the rest of them with Edgar.

As Edgar cruised the soft wind, he missed several chances to zero in on fallen prey. His mind was teeming with questions. These stories told by "Little Lamb" got under his skin in some strange way he didn't understand. They made him nervous. Each tale had some character, some surprising idea, that seemed to knock at the door of his broken heart—a door Edgar kept tightly locked. No one would ever get in there to hurt him again.

So why did he keep listening to the sheep?

Several times during the morning of storytelling, Edgar had wanted to ask Galya some questions, something, perhaps, that would allow him to get at the true message of these stories. But he held his tongue. Something forced him to stay hidden behind that raw, skeptical coating.

Edgar wanted his heart to stop hurting; that was the real truth. But he couldn't risk the disappointment that might come his way if he did something about it. A broken heart is a painful wound, but there is a kind of pain that is even worse—bringing this broken heart out in the open in a search for healing, and having the wound opened even deeper.

Edgar wanted to let Galya know he cared—he wanted to behave as a genuine friend just once—but he couldn't bring himself to do it. If only he could believe, if even just for a moment, that his dark and sad life had meaning, that a caring God was really in control. But the risk was too great. It was much safer to hide inside the ragged, spiny shell where no one could get through to hurt him. But more and more, he was feeling like a prisoner inside that shell.

The Sheep Tales made him think about breaking out, perhaps finding some shred of hope once again. It scared him to even think about it—and so he had flown away from Galya. As he took wing he began to harden himself, as he had done so many times before. He began erecting yet another protective wall around his heart. This would be the last of the Sheep Tales for him. And this would be the last of any friendship with a weak, gullible sheep.

Edgar suddenly became aware of an overwhelming smell of death that filled the air. He banked into a tight circle to catch the scent again and to get a bearing on his meal. He had not eaten since the day before, and he was hungry. It felt good to focus again on the simple chores of daily survival—a welcome relief after wrestling with the dangerous thoughts the Sheep Tales set loose within him.

Edgar followed the smell. He landed near a large carcass and began to feed. But no sooner had he begun than his head seemed to explode in a blast of light. His guard had been down, and it took the raven several seconds to realize he was being attacked.

He was fighting for his life too suddenly and desperately to even identify the savage creature now clawing at him. All he knew was that a vicious bird had swooped down on him from behind. Edgar tried to get his feet under him, but he was immediately knocked over. He felt the talons of his attacker slash sharply into his body.

In terrible pain, Edgar found himself
rolling down a steep hill until he came
to rest in a deep depression beneath
a rotting log, with the bigger bird
still lashing out at him.

He could hear the screech of his
attacker and see the bloodred thrusts
of its beak and talons. He didn't
know where he was. It seemed that
he had rolled into an opening too
small for his assailant to enter. He
could only huddle as close to the back
of his shelter as possible as his foe
screeched and tore at the ground, trying
to finish him off.

As he had many times before, yet again
Edgar longed for true eyesight. He had no
way of knowing what kind of bird was
attacking—but whatever it was, it
finally gave up. Edgar lay quietly until
he was sure the crisis had passed. It
was almost an hour before he
dared to stretch his wings and lift
his feet. He wasn't in good shape—
each time he moved his wings a
sharp pain erupted from a bleed-
ing wound in his chest. He was
grateful to realize he could still fly—
though he would have to wait. Light was
fading, and because of his eyes Edgar could not fly in the dark. There
was nothing to do but settle into his little haven of safety and wait
for the morning.

There would be no sleep tonight. Edgar felt very alone, with no
companion but his own thoughts. And one of them now seemed to
fill his mind.

Edgar had wondered for a long time if life was even worth living. Since his mother's death, he had toyed more than once with the thought of ending his miserable existence. But the awful attack had made one thing very clear: Edgar wanted to live. But he wanted more than just to exist—to eat, sleep, and scowl at life. He wanted his life to mean something.

Edgar needed something to hang on to—something that had meaning and offered answers. Galya's beliefs were easy to ridicule, but there was no one on earth who gave him the time Galya did; no one else had been so patient with him. Maybe that's why he had to admit to himself that he liked to be near Galya. He realized that he really did want to hear more of the Sheep Tales—especially if there were others like the story of Daniel, who had been protected from the lions by angels.

As Edgar flew home the next morning, he even dared to wonder if an angel like the one that protected Daniel had protected him from his attacker. Then he remembered the lion named Dandy, and he began to laugh. He had to land twice because he couldn't fly and laugh so uncontrollably at the same time. He was still laughing when he reached Galya's pen.

This time it was Edgar's turn to tell a story. Galya seemed delighted to listen, and he was spellbound as Edgar recounted the previous night's adventure. Actually, it was a slightly embellished version of what really happened. As a matter of fact, the more Edgar talked, the more thrilling and the less accurate it became. In Edgar's final version of the story, he had mercilessly torn out the eyes of his attacker, leaving the poor creature to stumble blindly through the woods. According to Edgar, he had spent the night eluding other assailants as he tried to hunt down the winged beast that had attacked him.

Edgar assured Galya that if he had only had normal eyesight, whatever it was that attacked him would have been dead this morning. He even speculated that it might have been a rouge rooster that attacked him. (Edgar hated roosters!) When Galya laughed at such a silly notion, Edgar assured him that whatever it was, it was at least as big as a rooster.

In the fresh air and daylight, much of Edgar's new resolve from the night before had slipped away. In many ways he was just the same old Edgar. He kept silent about the thoughts that had come to him as he lay huddled under the log, and he certainly didn't share the feelings he had acknowledged about his true friend, Galya.

Galya watched in silence as Edgar found a soft corner of the pen and wriggled down into the dirt. He fluttered his wings so that a fine dust rose all around him. When the dust settled, much of it was on Edgar. He looked like a dust ball with wings. "How's your supply of stories holding up?" asked Edgar in his usual sarcastic tone. "Got any more?"

A Great Fish Tale

> *The word of the LORD came to Jonah son of Amittai: "Go to the great city of Nineveh and preach against it, because its wickedness has come up before me."*
>
> *But Jonah ran away from the LORD and headed for Tarshish. He went down to Joppa, where he found a ship bound for that port.*[1]

GLUBBER

A familiar, ominous rumble interrupted the melodic chirps and pings of conversation between the huge whales that swam near the bottom of the ocean. For a moment the depths were silent, as if waiting. Then it came with an unsophisticated glub. Glubber hoped no one noticed the huge bubble that escaped from his mouth and divided into hundreds of smaller bubbles as it made its way from the cool depths of the sea to the surface two hundred feet above. If the others did notice, they didn't show it. They resumed their chatter as though nothing had happened.

Glubber's very first act as a living mammal had been a belch. His mother had originally named him Phinehas,

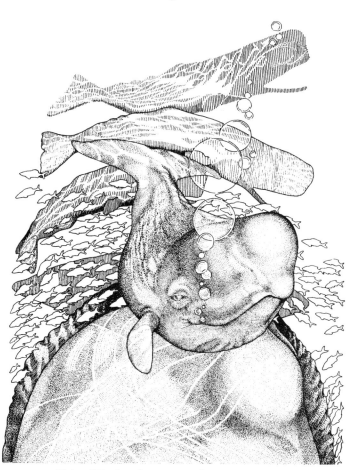

but because of his affliction he got nicknamed Glubber—and that's all they called him for the rest of his life. His mother had rolled and squealed in delight the first time it had happened. Proudly she had nudged him toward the others in the pod, so they could watch his little body convulse and see the trickle of air escape. Somehow, every time Glubber breached the surface, he would not only take air into his lungs but also gulp a huge amount into his stomach. Then, as he dove to the indigo depths, the air would compress and the need to belch would become irresistible.

In the beginning it was fun. Glubber made a game of chasing the bubbles to the surface. His beautiful body would come completely out of the water as he tried to catch them at the last moment. Then, as he crashed back into the water, he would wonder at the mystery of it all. Where had the bubbles gone? He also carried back with him another huge gulp of air that would produce the next batch of bubbles. It didn't matter how deep Glubber swam; anyone on the surface could have followed his progress just by watching for the bubbles.

This time no one paid attention, except for his mother, and she said nothing. Her baby's air problem had ceased being cute years ago.

When Glubber was young, he had suffered cruel teasing. Whales his own age often rejected him. On other occasions he was the focal point of their games. More than once they had used their combined strength to force him into shallow water. Then they would gather just offshore to laugh at his struggle to get back into water deep enough to ensure his survival. The longer he struggled, the more air he gulped. The more air he gulped, the more he belched—and the more fun they could have at his expense.

For Glubber it was no fun. He was terrified. He knew that someday the outgoing tide could leave him stranded and he would die.

One day the gang of young whales forced Glubber into an underwater cave and wouldn't let him out. They took turns guarding the entrance until finally he panicked. Desperate for air, he forced his way through their barricade and shot to the surface to breathe. The belch that resulted from that breach was heard for miles. The other whales had erupted in laughter at the size of the bubble, wagering that it could sink a small fishing boat.

Glubber carried physical scars on his body as evidence of the cruelty he had suffered at the whims of his pod mates. But it was the inner scars, formed from years of bullying, that shaped Glubber's life. He harbored so much bitterness for so long that his stomach became his second "body problem." He often couldn't keep down a meal, which only added to his humiliation.

He was older now, and the teasing had stopped long ago. Most of Glubber's friends had grown up, and they were friendlier to him. They even invited him to their social gatherings. But his fear and insecurity had forever made him a loner. Glubber wasn't sure his cohorts deserved a second chance, and if they did, he didn't know if he could forgive them.

The pod moved from feeding grounds to breeding areas, and as they journeyed for miles across the beautiful ocean floor, following the currents that carried their food, one lone whale always trailed like a sad, dark shadow. Bubbles trailed from the corner of his mouth, and his stomach rumbled in queasy unrest.

As the morning dawned on a day Glubber would never forget, his own stomach awakened him from slumber. He swam slowly away from the pod. Never had he felt so sick. He didn't notice the strange shadow on the surface, nor could he know that the object casting the shadow was going to have such a great impact on his life. It was stormy on the surface; Glubber could tell from the murkiness of the water. On calm days he could look up and see the surface like a glittering mirror. But today the brightness of the sun had been replaced by a foreboding darkness. The surface was a cauldron of boiling shapes.

Glubber's stomach rebelled with a monstrous belch. His largest bubble yet had erupted, beginning to make its way to the restless surface. He watched it for a moment as it rose. This one was different—it didn't split into smaller bubbles. The higher it rose, the faster it moved and the larger it expanded. This bubble was huge—and Glubber was suddenly tired of the whole thing. Too many years of humiliation; too many stomachaches! Glubber lost his temper.

The bubble had already risen a quarter of the way to the surface when he snapped. He surged upward toward it, twisting his immense body sharply. In the past, he might well have chased the bubble merely out of a playful spirit. Now it was frustration and fury that caused him to expend a ton of energy chasing a single helpless sphere of air.

After paying the fare, [Jonah] went aboard and sailed for Tarshish to flee from the LORD.

Then the LORD sent a great wind on the sea, and such a violent storm arose that the ship threatened to break up. All the sailors were afraid and each cried out to his own god. And they threw the cargo into the sea to lighten the ship.

But Jonah had gone below deck, where he lay down and fell into a deep sleep. The captain went to him and said, "How can you sleep? Get up and call on your god! Maybe he will take notice of us, and we will not perish."

Then the sailors said to each other, "Come, let us cast lots to find out who is responsible for this calamity." They cast lots and the lot fell on Jonah.

So they asked him, "Tell us, who is responsible for making all this trouble for us? What do you do? Where do you come from? What is your country? From what people are you?"

He answered, "I am a Hebrew and I worship the LORD, the God of heaven, who made the sea and the land."

This terrified them and they asked, "What have you done?" (They knew he was running away from the LORD, because he had already told them so.)

The sea was getting rougher and rougher. So they asked him, "What should we do to you to make the sea calm down for us?"

"Pick me up and throw me into the sea," he replied, "and it will become calm. I know that it is my fault that this great storm has come upon you."

Instead, the men did their best to row back to land. But they could not, for the sea grew even wilder than before. Then they cried to the LORD, "O LORD, please do not let us die for taking this man's life. Do not hold us accountable for killing an innocent man, for you, O LORD, have done as you pleased." Then they took Jonah and threw him overboard, and the raging sea grew calm. At this the men greatly feared the LORD, and they offered a sacrifice to the LORD and made vows to him.

But the LORD provided a great fish to swallow Jonah.[2]

Within seconds, Glubber's powerful frame was moving at incredible speed. Tears blended with the salty seawater as he began to overtake the bubble. Just beneath the surface, he gave a final thrust of his massive tail and opened his mouth. At the very last second, he thought he saw a strange creature reflected in the bubble. A jolt of fear shot through his body, but it was too late. Fear only elevated his adrenaline as Glubber broke the surface, and he shot twenty-five feet into the air. Time seemed to stand still as he hung

At the very last second, he thought he saw a strange creature
reflected in the bubble.

there, at the height of his arc. As if in a dream, he returned to the water in slow motion. In his panic, Glubber gulped a huge volume of air—and something else as well.

The surface exploded as Glubber crashed back into the water. His anger was replaced by terror, for something was choking him. During his moment in midair, he had caught a glimpse of a boat and a creature—and the creature had been scooped into his belly! Glubber knew this was the kind of creature called a *man*. He swam in sheer panic, trying to get his throat clear so he could breathe again. Near the bottom, he swallowed hard. That did the trick; the object dislodged from Glubber's throat and settled into his belly—a belly filled with air.

Glubber had sunk to a new low point in his life. Since birth, he'd always been on the move. Even in the darkest moments of his life, he had cruised along just above the ocean floor. But now he settled to the bottom and came to a grinding halt. His fit of rage had done nothing to make him feel better. His bitterness weighed on him like a great iron anchor from one of the men's ships. The light of hope began to seep from his soul.

Glubber began to think dark thoughts. If he couldn't forgive, then he couldn't be forgiven. He hadn't been able to forgive the whales who had bullied him, and he could find no relief from the pain he felt all the time. In his youth, his mother had been there for him. Even the bullies had actually tried to offer friendship. They were gone now, too.

Glubber was alone, drowning in misery at the bottom of the sea.

Something stirred in his stomach. But it wasn't a belch this time; it wasn't a stomach cramp, either—the man was moving around inside him. It wasn't terribly painful, but it did make Glubber feel sick to his stomach. Then he heard a faint voice—it was unmistakable—and somehow he could understand what was being said.

From inside the fish Jonah prayed to the LORD his God. He said:

"In my distress I called to the LORD,
and he answered me.

From the depths of the grave I called for help,
  and you listened to my cry.
You hurled me into the deep,
  into the very heart of the seas,
  and the currents swirled about me;
all your waves and breakers
  swept over me.
I said, 'I have been banished
  from your sight;
yet I will look again
  toward your holy temple.'
The engulfing waters threatened me,
  the deep surrounded me;
  seaweed was wrapped around my head.
To the roots of the mountains I sank down;
  the earth beneath barred me in forever.
But you brought my life up from the pit,
  O LORD, my God.

"When my life was ebbing away,
  I remembered you, LORD,
and my prayer rose to you,
  to your holy temple.

"Those who cling to worthless idols
  forfeit the grace that could be theirs.
But I, with a song of thanksgiving,
  will sacrifice to you.
What I have vowed I will make good.
  Salvation comes from the LORD."[3]

Glubber let his great body drift with the current; then he began to swim with new energy. Those final words had stirred something within him. He knew nothing about the man who uttered the prayer. It seemed that other men had dumped him into the sea. Glubber was reminded of the occasions when he had been forced ashore by other whales, so he knew something of what the man must have been feeling.

But it also seemed that the man had hurt his Creator deeply. How could someone facing certain death say, "Salvation comes from the LORD"?

Glubber had never known anything larger than himself. After all, what could be bigger than a whale? No creature in the sea had ever challenged him. But this wasn't a cheerful thought. It only made him feel more helpless and alone. If there was nothing bigger than he was, to whom could he turn?

But the man's prayer suggested there *was* someone greater after all.

The waters were growing shallower as Glubber cruised through, and he turned up the speed. His mind was churning as fast as his stomach. He knew he had to time this just right—or the tide could leave him stranded.

Glubber was turning green when he exploded from the water and slid up into a tidal pool, the sound of pebbles grinding beneath his weight. But that sound was buried beneath another one: whale-retching.

This is not a sound that can be described . . .

•　•　•

"Describe it!" Edgar demanded, chuckling as Galya shook his head in exasperation.

"The Great Book gives no description of this sound," said Galya, "but it clearly tells us what happened."

•　•　•

And the LORD commanded the fish, and it vomited Jonah onto dry land.

Then the word of the LORD came to Jonah a second time: "Go to the great city of Nineveh and proclaim to it the message I give you."[4]

Glubber heard the Voice speak to the man he now felt being cradled against his massive flukes.

Apparently the man had disobeyed his Master's instructions. Yet the Creator had given him a second chance. The prayer from the

Glubber was turning green when he exploded from the water and slid up into a tidal pool, the sound of pebbles grinding beneath his weight. But that sound was buried beneath another one: whale-retching.

floor of the sea had ignited Glubber's hope, and now these hopes were fanned into flame. Maybe forgiveness *was* real. Perhaps it was something he could experience; perhaps it was something he could do.

The tide turned. The Master of the waves was not done with Glubber. Gradually the incoming tide lifted his own crushing weight and floated him once again. Glubber swam to deeper waters, but he didn't dive to the cool depths. Instead, he cruised for hour after hour in the warm waters near the surface. Glubber had some thinking to do.

• • •

"That can't be all!" Edgar exclaimed. "A fish vomits on the beach and then wants to think about it? That's your entire story?"

"No, that's not my entire story, and you know it," Galya responded. "It's all about forgiveness."

Edgar suddenly became more serious.

Galya knew two things about Edgar: Edgar blamed God for his mother's death, and he wouldn't discuss forgiveness. It was amazing the raven had even bothered to stay around for the whole story.

Galya wanted Edgar to hear the rest of the tale, so he tried to lighten the mood a little. "Edgar, when I take a breath, it doesn't necessarily mean the story is over. Sometimes it just means I need to breathe."

"Then take a deep one and get on with it," Edgar snapped. "I wish your story were as deep as your breath."

Edgar was nervous, and it showed. Galya knew the next part of the Sheep Tales would ruffle his feathers.

As the Worm Turns

EARL

When Jonah was called to go to the city of Nineveh, he wasn't too thrilled about it. Neither was Earl, who was called at the same time.

Earl was a worm, and Nineveh was a fishing town. This didn't seem like a happy combination, especially since Earl came from a rare line of worms. He certainly didn't want the family line to become scarcer on his account.

God sent Earl to a place known as The Crossing, where two pathways intersected on a barren hillside just east of the city. The ground there supported little vegetation—only rocks and a few scattered remnants of what was once a cedar forest. But at the point where the trails crossed, there was a small patch of fertile soil. An underground spring ran beneath the ground, and though it didn't bubble up over the surface, it kept the soil moist all around it. Young boys knew it as the perfect spot to dig for worms.

And it was the very spot God had selected for Earl's mission.

Earl wasn't offered any details, only that he should head for
The Crossing and wait for further orders. Needless to say, when Earl
heard the Voice speak the shocking instructions, he tried to talk
his way out of the whole thing. (One reason Earl's line was so rare
was that it had talked itself almost into extinction.)

He argued for several minutes before it occurred to him that the
Voice wasn't listening. Then he started to crawl—not toward Nineveh, but in the precise opposite direction. On purpose the worm
had turned, but down the wrong road.

Earl had traveled no more than a few inches when a large raven
landed directly in his path. The bird hopped directly toward him,
pausing to turn its head from side to side, as though he couldn't quite
decide which end to eat first.

• • •

"I think I'm going to like this story," Edgar interjected with a
wicked chuckle. Galya continued, without even acknowledging
the comment.

• • •

Earl closed all his eyes and braced himself for the inevitable.

• • •

Edgar jumped to his feet. "A worm doesn't have eyes," he
protested. "I have eaten more worms than you will ever see in a lifetime. Not one of them had eyes."

"According to the Sheep Tales, this was a *rare* worm, and he
had lots of eyes," Galya countered. "Besides, how would *you* know?
You can hardly see what you're eating."

Galya was immediately sorry for the insensitivity of his comment, but Edgar didn't seem to be offended. The raven started to
answer, "My mother told me . . ." Then his voice trailed off.

"It isn't important," Galya continued. "What *is* important is that
a worm played a central role in this story, as the Great Book assures
us. What is also important is the *message* of a Sheep Tale, not all its
tiny details. Just relax and enjoy the story!"

Edgar was still grumbling about worms and eyes as Galya continued.

• • •

Earl waited for what seemed like an eternity. Slowly he opened one eye at a time. When he could finally see again, the raven was still standing there, only inches away, staring intently at him.

Earl began to chatter. If he could make small talk, perhaps he could gain enough time to work out a way to escape. The raven either didn't hear him or wasn't listening, and took a stealthy step toward Earl. But at that very moment, a quiet voice spoke—the exact same one that had instructed Earl to go to Nineveh. The Voice whispered only two words: *Turn around.*

Earl didn't have to think very long before obeying the Voice. Never taking his eyes from the raven, Earl began to slowly shift one segment of his body at a time. It took almost half an hour for him to maneuver his tail backward without moving his head. It seemed very important to go slowly. Any sudden movements might provoke an attack from the raven.

Finally, all of his body except for the head was lined up away from the raven and pointing toward Nineveh. It now seemed like a wise idea to obey the Voice and to make a trip to that city.

Earl shivered fearfully, turned his head, and began to crawl away, fully expecting a sharp raven's beak to pluck him from the path at any moment. At first he crawled slowly, but when nothing happened, he became more confident. Earl pulled out all the stops and moved as fast as he could go. As a worm, he had only two speeds—slow and really slow—and there wasn't much difference between the two. He only looked back once—to see how closely the raven might be following him. But when he arched his head backward to take a peek, the raven was nowhere to be seen.

For the rest of the journey, Earl didn't stop or look back again.

Jonah obeyed the word of the LORD and went to Nineveh. Now Nineveh was a very important city—a visit required three days. On the first day, Jonah started into the city. He proclaimed:

"Forty more days and Nineveh will be overturned." The Ninevites believed God. They declared a fast, and all of them, from the greatest to the least, put on sackcloth.

When the news reached the king of Nineveh, he rose from his throne, took off his royal robes, covered himself with sackcloth and sat down in the dust. Then he issued a proclamation in Nineveh:

"By the decree of the king and his nobles:

Do not let any man or beast, herd or flock, taste anything; do not let them eat or drink. But let man and beast be covered with sackcloth. Let everyone call urgently on God. Let them give up their evil ways and their violence. Who knows? God may yet relent and with compassion turn from his fierce anger so that we will not perish."

When God saw what they did and how they turned from their evil ways, he had compassion and did not bring upon them the destruction he had threatened.

But Jonah was greatly displeased and became angry. He prayed to the LORD, "O LORD, is this not what I said when I was still at home? That is why I was so quick to flee to Tarshish. I knew that you are a gracious and compassionate God, slow to anger and abounding in love, a God who relents from sending calamity. Now, O LORD, take away my life, for it is better for me to die than to live."

But the LORD replied, "Have you any right to be angry?"[1]

When the Voice had first sent Earl to The Crossing, he was actually within several hundred yards of it—yet it took him the entire time span of Jonah's adventure to reach his destination. As he approached the place, he could immediately feel the moisture in the ground beneath him. A man walking along the path might not notice the slight change in vegetation or the darker color of the ground. But worms were made to notice such things.

As Earl crawled the last several yards, a man came down the path and flopped on the ground right at the intersection of the two trails. Earl halted abruptly. Could this man be hunting for worms? Earl wanted no part of that. He quickly burrowed under a clump of soil and peeked out to see what would happen next.

The man didn't seem to be planning a calm fishing trip. He was shouting into the sky and gesturing wildly. Pointing down the hill toward the city of Nineveh, the man was demanding that God destroy it immediately. He ranted about how long the people of Nineveh had been up to their evil tricks. He pointed out how unfair it was for them to be let off the hook on the basis of one brief moment of repentance. (Earl shivered again at the mere mention of the word *hook*.)

The man behaved as though he was not going to budge from that hillside until he saw the city go up in flames. He sat down and mumbled angrily to himself, rising only to drag a cedar stump to his little spot. He added some rocks and a few pieces of burned wood, and then, sweating profusely, he sat down. The man obviously needed some protection from the hot sun.

> Jonah went out and sat down at a place east of the city. There he made himself a shelter, sat in its shade and waited to see what would happen to the city. Then the LORD God provided a vine and made it grow up over Jonah to give shade for his head to ease his discomfort, and Jonah was very happy about the vine.[2]

Earl had never seen anything like it in all his life. All his eyes were bulging as the vine eased out of the ground. He could actually see it getting bigger. By the end of the day, its enormous leaves almost covered the man—who had finally stopped grumbling and was settling back in the coolness of the shade.

That night, as Earl listened to the man snoring, a hundred questions robbed him of sleep: *Why am I here? What does the Voice want from me? What possible mission could a worm accomplish?*

Earl had listened to the man's description of things, and he had to admit it was strange that God had so fully forgiven those people down the hill. Everyone for miles around knew about their cruelty and their evil deeds. The way Earl saw it, somebody should have to pay. The man had a point; it just didn't seem right. Perhaps tomorrow this God would remember the sins of Nineveh and send down bolts of fire to even the score. It might be a sight worth seeing.

When dawn was just about to break, Earl was dozing. That's when the Voice came for the final time, and Earl received his orders. It was nothing like the spectacular feat he had imagined. Earl had dreamed of the Voice enlarging him to a towering stature, like the vine, so that he would be the world's most gigantic worm; or making him speedy, so it wouldn't take him so long to cover short distances. He had even wondered if he, as the "monster worm," would be called on to devour the city of Nineveh. That could be fun!

As it turned out, his job was much simpler—and not at all unpleasant. Earl hadn't eaten for two days, and he'd worked up an incredible appetite. By the time the sun reached its zenith, his mission had been accomplished.

But at dawn the next day God provided a worm, which chewed the vine so that it withered. When the sun rose, God provided a scorching east wind, and the sun blazed on Jonah's head so that he grew faint. He wanted to die, and said, "It would be better for me to die than to live."

But God said to Jonah, "Do you have a right to be angry about the vine?"

"I do," he said. "I am angry enough to die."

But the LORD said, "You have been concerned about this vine, though you did not tend it or make it grow. It sprang up overnight and died overnight. But Nineveh has more than a hundred and twenty thousand people who cannot tell their right hand from their left, and many cattle as well. Should I not be concerned about that great city?"[3]

As Earl started back toward his home, he reflected again on the evil deeds of the people of Nineveh. The list of crimes was enormous. They were people without mercy, yet that's exactly what they had received. What an amazing God to forgive so much and so completely!

As it turned out, his job was much simpler—and not at all unpleasant.

Earl should have been watching where he was going, but he was deep in thought. He never saw the boys coming. By the time he felt the ground shaking with their footsteps, it was too late; Earl was dangling high above the ground, securely held in the grimy fingers of a young boy.

Earl was tossed unceremoniously into a basket with dozens of other worms of every kind. Many of them were quite unsavory characters with whom Earl had nothing in common. Some had no legs or eyes. But they did have one thing in common: They were all going fishing.

Earl needed someone to talk to. He babbled on and on about his great adventure, but no one was listening. Or if they were listening, they weren't talking.

At least Earl's dream of traveling quickly was coming true—the boys made it to the seashore in a fraction of the time it would have taken Earl. Once there, they climbed on a crude raft and pushed off on their expedition.

For hours, Earl listened as the boys laughed and chattered and caught fish. Every so often, the basket lid would disappear and sunlight would stream in, followed by a grubby little hand. Earl would wriggle up under a lip at the edge of the basket and close all his eyes except two—one to watch the hand, and one to make sure he kept his grip on the lip. The dirty fingers would grope for a worm, then the lid would fall shut and Earl could relax for another moment or two.

Another worm had just been seized, and Earl had fallen back into the main part of the basket—when the lid suddenly flew open again.

No! It was too soon! The grubby fingers closed around him.

This time Earl knew the end was near. He knew all about fishing. Horror stories about hooks and worms had been impressed on him from his earliest days. He knew that if the hook didn't kill him, a fish would certainly do the job.

It all happened so quickly. He saw the hook approaching his body. He closed every eye as tightly as it would go—he had absolutely no desire to peek. Earl shuddered, then gasped as a cold chill spread across every section of him. Is this what death felt like?

Earl opened his eyes as he slowly sank beneath the waves. Afraid he would not be able to bear the sight of seeing himself skewered, he twisted around to examine his body. *There was no hook!*

Somehow he had been dropped into the water. He might drown, but at least he wouldn't suffer the humiliation of dying as a piece of bait. He turned toward shore and began swimming "the crawl." It was the same motion he used to propel himself across the ground—only slower.

But suddenly Earl was confronted with the biggest creature he'd ever seen. So this was how it would end. He had been saved from the hook only to become a snack for some ugly, overgrown sea monster. Earl didn't move a muscle. He heard a strange *glub,* and a huge bubble emerged from the mouth of the monster. The bubble was heading for the surface. Earl began to beg frantically for mercy.

Glubber gazed curiously at the worm that hung suspended in the water before him. He had never seen such a creature before. There were worms in the ocean, but he had never seen one with legs and eyes. There was a sound coming from the worm, but it was so soft that he couldn't make it out.

Glubber eased closer until the motionless little worm was only inches from his right eye. Now he could just barely make out the sounds coming from the worm. The little creature was speaking, and Glubber was astonished that he could understand its language.

The worm was shouting, "I am Earl. Have mercy on me, just as God had mercy on Nineveh!"

Since Glubber had no evil intentions toward the worm, he was willing to consider the plea for mercy. However, he was very curious about Earl's comment about Nineveh. Just recently, Glubber had vomited a man onto the beach, and he had clearly heard a voice mention that city. "Go to the great city of Nineveh and proclaim to it the message I give you," it had said. Ever since, Glubber had found himself wondering what the message was all about. This just might be his chance to find out.

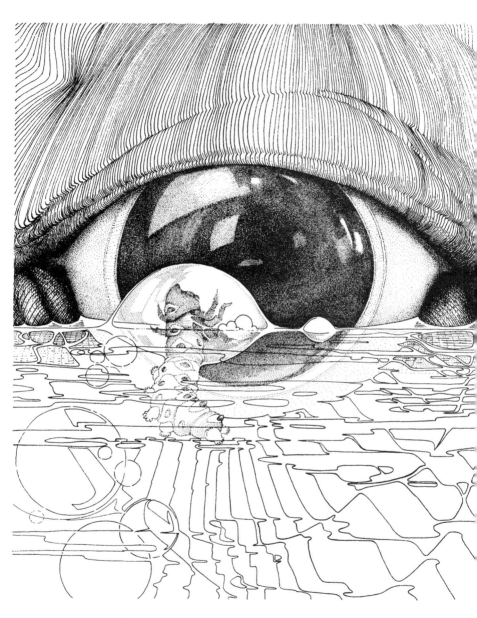

Glubber eased closer until the motionless little worm was
only inches from his right eye.

"Tell me about God's mercy on Nineveh!" he demanded with all the menace he could muster.

Earl began to talk—something he was very good at. As a matter of fact, an hour later he was *still* talking. He told Glubber of Jonah's mission to warn the Ninevites of impending judgment. He told of their repentance, and how God was moved to forgive them and spare their city. Earl went on in great detail about Jonah's anger at God's mercy, and he related every minute detail of his own role in the whole affair.

Most of the time when Earl got into his talking, his listeners would fall asleep or slowly begin moving away. But this time was different. The more Earl talked, the more fascinated Glubber became. Since the day he had heard the prayer that came from the pit of his stomach, a seed of hope had begun to grow in Glubber's heart. Now he discovered that God, the Creator, had planted that seed. If such a God could find it in Himself to forgive the horrible deeds of Nineveh, then maybe...just maybe...

As Earl prattled on about the boys who had captured him, Glubber began to see the face of every sea creature who had ever mocked or tortured him. The names and faces paraded through his mind one by painful one. He knew all the details, because he had brooded bitterly over them for so long. He had fed and nurtured those memories until even the most trivial offenses had grown into monsters. He had clutched them tightly in anticipation of the day when some stroke of revenge on his part would finally set them free.

Now Glubber realized that *he* was the one who needed to be set free. He had been held captive by his own bitterness and hatred. He needed to forgive.

Somewhere at the edge of his mind, Glubber could still hear Earl droning on and on. He was asking something about catching a ride to shore. But Glubber's attention was focused on a single thought: *The God who forgave the people of Nineveh could forgive his own stupidity and bitterness.* He now felt certain of that fact, and it changed everything. He had so much to learn, and so much to do. As Earl continued to babble—now he had moved on to an account of his humble upbringing in a neighborhood marsh—Glubber slowly turned toward the open sea and began to swim away.

Earl's voice had faded into silence when Glubber paused momentarily in the water. For several minutes, he sat quietly, suspended near the surface. Then he turned around and looked at Earl. He could see that Earl was gesturing. (Worms rarely gesture, but when they do, it is very obvious, even from a distance.) Glubber could tell that the strange little worm was still speaking.

So, with one swift motion, Glubber darted forward and swallowed Earl.

• • •

"Wait!" Edgar screeched in protest. "Why didn't the *raven* eat the little blabbermouth? It would have been a real meal for a raven. But for a whale? Why, it'd be like you eating a quarter of a kernel of corn. Glubber must have been really hard up for food."

Galya tried to explain, but Edgar blundered on. "Anyway, I was just starting to like the creepy little crawler—then the fish uses him for a snack. Galya, your stories are in need of some serious rewriting."

Galya just sat there, shaking his head. "Are you done?" he asked.

"As a matter of fact—no!" snapped Edgar. "But Earl is done! He just became a monster morsel! Fish food! A Sheep Tale tidbit!

"Are you done *now*?" Galya asked again.

"Yeah, yeah, I'm done. I just think it's stupid that Glubber ate the worm, that's all." Edgar turned away, disgusted.

"Just pipe down and listen," Galya commanded. "The story's not quite done."

• • •

Immediately Glubber's stomach began to rumble. He was not swimming out to sea—but toward the shore. Earl had brought the best news Glubber had ever heard; the least he could do was to give him a ride back to the beach. Earl, like Jonah before him, had his second chance coming up—coming up rather violently. The worm would smell like fish vomit; he would be waterlogged and exhausted—but all that mattered was that he would be free!

Mission accomplished, Glubber swam joyfully toward the open ocean. He was praying for forgiveness and for the strength to forgive others. He was thinking about a life without the burdens of bitterness and resentment.

It wouldn't be long now before he, too, would be free.

• • •

Galya stared at Edgar, waiting for some kind of response. When none came, Galya spoke. "*Now* are you happier with the ending?"

"I might be—that is, if the storyteller had any skill at all," Edgar sniped.

"As I keep telling you, the important thing is the *point* of the story," Galya declared. "Did you get the point?"

"Hmmm," said Edgar, "let me think. Um, could it be, 'Don't eat worms on an empty stomach'?"

It was at times like this that Galya wondered if all this was worth it. He had enough on his mind without Edgar's sarcasm. Why even try to reach him if it was a hopeless task? Nothing was getting through. Finally Galya said, "It was about *forgiveness,* Edgar. In many ways, it's *all* about forgiveness."

Edgar said nothing. He knew he had overstepped his bounds, and he actually found himself worried that Galya might stop telling the stories.

Yet a part of him didn't want to hear any more of them. Edgar played dumb, but he knew well enough what the stories were about; he was simply incapable of admitting it to Galya. He was also incapable of taking hold of the truth, for it was a truth that called to him in the same way his mother's love did—and it frightened him terribly.

So Edgar chose to remain silent, frightened that Galya might not tell another story, and just as frightened that he might.

Galya walked to the far end of the pen and stretched, gazing closely at Edgar. Somehow, in spite of his brash exterior, he looked so lonely. For a fleeting instant, the eyes of the two creatures locked.

Galya sighed deeply, walked back toward his friend, and settled down again. He decided to give it one more try.

Galya walked to the far end of the pen and stretched, gazing closely at Edgar. Somehow, in spite of his brash exterior, he looked so lonely. For a fleeting instant, the eyes of the two creatures locked.

8 The Tower

SOCRATES

The rocky peaks shone like brilliant candles as the morning sun chased the shadows down the slope. Beldone relaxed on a bushy outcropping of rock known as The Tower. He smiled as he watched his mate and his young son grazing in the warm blanket of sunshine that covered the tiny mountain meadow.

Beldone was fond of this little corner of the hill country. It was tucked into a saddle between two craggy peaks, and it made a delightful place to spend a summer morning. It was also a dangerous place. A forest ridge ran up to it from the valley below, and predators could spring from the dark foliage at any time.

Beldone's eyes were happily fixed on his impressive son, who was now romping along with his mother. The young ram was a superb physical specimen and a quick learner. Every graceful little movement showed his mastery of the survival skills Beldone had taught him. His son would nibble a few bites, then his eyes would dart forward and backward, sizing up the landscape. Only after a careful study of the surrounding area would he lower his head for another bite.

Any ram in the mountain country would have proudly claimed such a bright and healthy son. Beldone had named him Socrates after his grandfather. The old ram had lived among men for the first part of his life. His name was known far and wide, established on the dark, windy night when he had fought off a lion as the rest of the flock huddled in fear. When the battle was over, Socrates had a deep wound that ran from his shoulder to the corner of his left eye. His attacker had gotten the worst of it, however. When the battle was over, the lion lay dead at the feet of the bloodied but unbowed ram. Socrates had managed to use his mighty horns to crush the beast against a boulder.

Grandfather Socrates was plenty of trouble for his owner because he was always attempting to make a run to freedom. So there was little sorrow among the men when Socrates finally managed to escape and vanish into the hills. He walked away from the flock in broad daylight one afternoon and then sprinted away for all he was worth. There he met a fine ewe just as wild and independent as himself, and within a year their first son, Beldone, was born.

Beldone had learned one lesson from his father and had forcefully handed it down to young Socrates. The lesson was never to surrender or submit—not to anyone, not for anything. Beldone spoke constantly about independence and self-preservation, the highest goals of life. Beldone had lived proudly by that philosophy, and he was anxious to instill the same wisdom in his son. He had no time for the sacrifices and the acts of faith practiced among the flocks that dwelt with men.

Gods, angels, even shepherds—who needed them? Beldone taught his son that the sweat of his own brow would supply his every need. Be quick and be clever, he insisted, and you'll be safe from any danger life brings your way.

"The only god you will ever need is right here," Beldone said, nudging his son's head. "Use your mind. Some creatures believe in the God in the sky. But that makes them weak and dependent on something other than themselves. Don't fall for that foolishness, son, for it will only bring heartbreak. Your grandfather was too smart for men or their gods, and so are you."

Pride—Beldone was filled with it as he surveyed his little hillside kingdom. Pride in his freedom, in his accomplishments, in his intelligence. Everything he saw before him was a result of his own effort. And his handsome, self-reliant, self-confident son would pass it all on to future generations. Beldone closed his eyes and stretched.

A bleat from below shattered Beldone's moment of quiet self-congratulation. Socrates and his mother were running toward him at full speed. Behind them, charging low to the ground and quickly closing the gap, was the spotted blur of a lion. Instantly, Beldone was on his feet, springing forward to fight for his family. He had always assured his loved ones that as long as he lived, he would be there to defend them.

Beldone had to get between his family and the lion. The attacker would not be dealing with any easy prey, for he was facing the son of Socrates the Lion Killer. The same hot, impassioned blood flowed through Beldone's veins. The same wild rage propelled him in a mad rush toward the predator that threatened his family. If he had to, he would take the intruder down in his tracks and batter him to death.

Beldone reached Socrates and his mother as the lion had closed to within seventy yards. "Run to the rocks!" he shouted, without slowing down or taking his eyes from the lion. The cat seemed to be itching for a fight. In times past, Beldone's aggressive charge at an enemy would have surprised it. Head-to-head fighting is not the way of lions, who prefer pouncing on their prey from behind as it flees in panic. When faced with a head-to-head confrontation, the common response of a lion was a strategic but deadly game of thrust and parry, false charges and quick retreats.

Beldone had played this game many times, and in the end the foe had always decided to go after some easier target. Beldone could be crazed, fearless, and relentless. But now, as the last yards of turf disappeared between the ram and the lion, the big cat showed no intention of slowing down. Instead, he sped up and lowered his head.

Beldone smiled. This was going to be easier than he thought. He might have a challenge facing the claws of a lion, but this kitten's skull was no match for the crushing power of Beldone's horns. He lowered his head and braced for the collision—which never came.

At the last possible moment, the lion had sprung high in the air, completely over Beldone. He continued at full speed toward Socrates and his mom. The lion had been crafty, and this time Beldone's blind rage had betrayed him. As Beldone tried frantically to stop, his left front hoof buckled beneath him; he rolled for fifty feet before he could recover control. But as quickly as he could, he leaped to his feet again and began to race up the mountain.

A searing pain shot up Beldone's leg and nearly caused him to stumble. He realized that his leg was seriously wounded—and overtaking the lion in time to save his family was now out of the question. He could only watch in agony as the hungry cat drew closer to his prey.

Socrates was young and fast, and he ran harder than he had ever run before. If he hadn't caught sight of the lion before it charged, there would have been no hope. Even now, he wasn't certain he could make it to the cliffs before the speedier lion caught up to him. He passed The Tower, where only a few minutes before he had felt so secure under his father's watchful eye. Only a few more leaps would bring him to a place no lion could ever reach. But he carefully selected the right spot and pulled up.

Socrates had passed his mother about a hundred yards back; now he anxiously looked back to see where she was. He was horrified to see that she had veered away from the safety of the cliffs and was standing near The Tower—face-to-face with the lion. He knew it was the beginning of the old game that always ended in death.

The lion circled as Socrates' mother stood defiantly atop a small jumble of rocks. Beldone was valiantly struggling up the mountain with one leg dangling uselessly beneath him. Clearly it would be too late by the time he arrived.

A weak, pitiful bleat issued from Socrates' throat as he fell to the ground. The lion looked up to see the young ram lying on his back trembling, with his delicate, helpless legs kicking wildly. The hungry lion never hesitated. Years of instinct propelled him toward the easiest meal. The lion could taste the tender flesh of the young ram as he raced the final yards to his kill.

But with perfect timing, Socrates leaped suddenly to his feet again—and with two powerful bounds, he vaulted over a deep crevice and scrambled up a cliff. He had placed himself in just the right strategic position. His plan had worked.

Socrates could have crossed the cliff in seconds, but instead he paused on a tiny ledge. The lion stood helplessly only yards away, roaring in rage, for he knew he'd been fooled. He paced back and forth, searching furiously for a way to reach the meal that beckoned just beyond his reach. Socrates took a quick glance to be sure that his mother and father had hurried to safety. Then, with a final, mocking bleat at the lion, Socrates hopped easily up the cliff and disappeared over the top.

It was noon when the family was finally reunited in a familiar cave near the peak of the mountain. Beldone had no words to describe the pride he felt for his son. When everything seemed lost, Socrates had used his quick mind and his quick feet to save them all. No father had ever been so pleased and proud.

But Socrates was in a quieter mood. It wasn't pride but questions that filled his mind and his mouth. "Why must life carry so many dangers?" he wanted to know. "Why can't lions climb the same cliffs we climb? And what if the lion hadn't fallen for my trick?

Beldone had no words to describe the pride he felt for his son. When everything seemed lost, Socrates had used his quick mind and his quick feet to save them all. No father had ever been so pleased and proud.

Should I have been prepared to sacrifice my life to save my mother, if it had come to that?"

At the last question, Beldone bristled. "You ask too many questions, Socrates," he interrupted. "Sacrifice is never necessary for the strong. There's nothing worth dying for. You saved yourself today, and in the process you saved your mother. That's all that matters; let's put away our questions and celebrate our family. Let's celebrate you!"

They slept in the high crevice that night. In the moonlight, Beldone looked down on the shadows cast by The Tower and reflected on the day's excitement. As he had struggled up the mountain during the crisis, there had been one brief moment when Beldone had felt the paralyzing sting of despair. It was the first time in his life he had allowed any such emotion to invade his heart. Now he was ashamed that he had succumbed to such weakness. His own flesh and blood had proven that doubts and despair are unnecessary; strength and cunning alone mattered.

Beldone took a deep breath and closed his eyes. Despite it all, something seemed incomplete. He wondered why he would be robbed of complete satisfaction on such a victorious day. He wanted to offer his gratitude, but whom could he thank?

Socrates' grave questions had disturbed Beldone. He wanted to ease his son's mind, but he didn't like questions and deep thinking. As he finally drifted off to sleep, he could not know that many of the same questions were churning through the heart of a man in the valley far below.

The Lesson

God tested Abraham. He said to him, "Abraham!"

"Here I am," he replied.

Then God said, "Take your son, your only son, Isaac, whom you love, and go to the region of Moriah. Sacrifice him there as a burnt offering on one of the mountains I will tell you about."

Early the next morning Abraham got up and saddled his donkey. He took with him two of his servants and his son Isaac.

When he had cut enough wood for the burnt offering, he set out for the place God had told him about.[1]

Beldone considered carefully. The word had reached him that Abraham, the great shepherd, was coming this way, climbing the mountain. Beldone sent his friend Casper to check out the rumors. Beldone was curious to know what would bring Abraham this far up the mountain, though he certainly held no fear of the man. The valley shepherds had little interest in the wild mountain sheep. The elder Socrates had been a part of the flocks of men for years before he made his escape.

Even then, Beldone's father hadn't been driven to the mountains by fear. Why be afraid? An unsightly scar had made the elder ram a poor candidate for sacrifice. Old Socrates wasn't pure or flawless enough to go under the knife. Having nothing to fear, he could be wild and unruly, though he was always treated kindly by men.

No, it hadn't been fear that had chased Beldone's father to the hill country; only a simple longing for adventure. He had a proud spirit and an unquenchable craving for independence. He yearned to run free and wild—and as far as possible from prayers and God-talk.

Casper reported back the next day. During the night he had spoken with the donkey that accompanied the men. The loud, abrasive beast reported that Abraham was coming to the mountain for a sacrifice. This wasn't particularly surprising, but the news Beldone struggled to believe concerned the identity of the sacrifice. It was Abraham's own son Isaac—and at God's command!

Even for men and their strange God, this was difficult to take in. Abraham's family was well-known in the area, so even mountain sheep knew all about the old man and his son Isaac. The word was that God had miraculously provided this boy to Abraham and his wife, who was well beyond childbearing years. And everyone knew that Abraham was proud of Isaac, just as they knew that Beldone was proud of Socrates.

And they all knew about "the great promise." God, it was said, had given His word that a great flock of people would walk the earth

through Isaac's line. For years God had made Abraham and Sarah wait for this son. And now, before the young man himself had had any children, he was being cruelly reclaimed by God! It was difficult even for a skeptical ram to accept. But the donkey had given his assurance that it was true.

Could there be a more perfect lesson for Socrates? Beldone planned on taking advantage of old Abraham's expedition. He would take Socrates to see a living example of the misery that faith brings. The young ram could find out just how destructive it could be to believe in God. Who would worship such a cruel God? This would clinch the issue—Socrates would never be tempted toward the folly of faith after this lesson.

Beldone and Socrates made their way down the mountain and soon located the men coming up from below. They shadowed the party, always using the bushes and trees to keep from being seen. None of the men ever saw them, but the donkey knew they were there. They had caught her eye on several occasions. The shepherds emerged from the trees at about the same place the lion had initiated his attack two days before.

When Abraham reached the high meadow, he lifted his hand and pointed to the dense, brush-covered ledge. "The Tower," whispered Beldone to Socrates.

> On the third day Abraham looked up and saw the place in the distance. He said to his servants, "Stay here with the donkey while I and the boy go over there. We will worship and then we will come back to you."[2]

As Abraham started toward The Tower, Beldone and Socrates made their way down and then back up around the meadow, all the while sticking to heavy cover. Beldone guessed that Abraham would be heading for the very spot Beldone had lay the morning the lion attacked. He knew of an especially dense tangle of brush that would hide them but at the same time give them a close view of everything that happened. Socrates would have a front-row seat to the most important lesson of his life. He would see that whatever god Abraham followed was not one that could be trusted. He would see that nothing is worth sacrifice. He would come away knowing that the highest power on earth was his own body and will. After this Socrates would be self-sufficient; he would never waste his time thinking about gods.

> Abraham took the wood for the burnt offering and placed it on his son Isaac, and he himself carried the fire and the knife. As the two of them went on together, Isaac spoke up and said to his father Abraham, "Father?"
>
> "Yes, my son?" Abraham replied.
>
> "The fire and wood are here," Isaac said, "but where is the lamb for the burnt offering?"
>
> Abraham answered, "God himself will provide the lamb for the burnt offering, my son." And the two of them went on together.[3]

The brush that surrounded The Tower was thicker and more snarled than anywhere on the mountain. It grew from the hundreds of fractures in the rock. The gnarled bases twisted in every direction, interlocking with other branches to form an almost impenetrable mass. Beldone was breathing heavily when he finally forced his way to a good vantage point. The place where Beldone had lay only days before was two or three bounds from where he lay now. Finally he could hear the men coming.

He had guessed right! This was the place where the sacrifice would occur. It was the only open area on The Tower. In order to reach it, Abraham and Isaac had to climb to the left, above the brush. It was there that a small corridor in the thicket provided access to the overlook. As Abraham and Isaac passed through the corridor and into the open, the two men walked within a few feet of where Beldone and Socrates lay concealed. Beldone whispered into Socrates' ear to lie still and be silent.

When they reached the place God had told him about, Abraham built an altar there and arranged the wood on it. He bound his son Isaac and laid him on the altar, on top of the wood. Then he reached out his hand and took the knife to slay his son.[4]

Beldone heard Socrates' breath catch in his throat. Anger and disgust swept over the father ram until he trembled with indignation. What kind of God would make such a cruel demand, while turning His back on a promise? And for that matter, what fool would make *any* kind of sacrifice to such a deceitful God, let alone the sacrifice of his own son?

It disturbed Beldone to be showing his son the horrible scene that was playing out before their eyes, but it had to be done. This was a hard lesson that *had* to be learned.

But the angel of the LORD called out to him from heaven, "Abraham! Abraham!"

"Here I am," he replied.

"Do not lay a hand on the boy," he said. "Do not do anything to him. Now I know that you fear God, because you have not withheld from me your son, your only son."[5]

When the voice came, it seemed to come out of nowhere—and everywhere. The moment had been filled with high tension already, but the sudden intervention of the angel caused Socrates to gasp and try to leap to his feet. But he was knocked down immediately by a thick branch over his head. Beldone instantly heaved his body backward, but the thick foliage, chosen for purposes of hiding, now worked against him. His horns became tangled in the thick undergrowth; he could not stand to his feet. He was trapped.

Beldone thrashed with all his might, but with each move the tangled branches gripped his horns even tighter. Socrates was also thrashing helplessly, trying to escape, but his father's body blocked the way they had come—the only path to safety. Beldone's worst fear was confirmed when he glanced up and found himself looking directly into the eyes of Abraham.

> Abraham looked up and there in a thicket he saw a ram caught by its horns.[6]

Beldone knew that if he continued to struggle, his son would not be able to escape.

The father ram had to decide quickly. In a hoarse whisper, he commanded Socrates to lie still. Beldone moved as far forward as he could and pressed his heaving body sideways against the brush. He spoke no words to Socrates; no words were needed. Their eyes met for one brief, final instant.

Socrates slammed headfirst into the small opening his father had created. After a brief struggle of frenzied writhing, he slipped past his trapped father and disappeared into the thicket behind him.

Once Socrates was gone, Beldone struggled until he had no energy left to give. Then he waited.

> [Abraham] went over and took the ram and sacrificed it as a burnt offering instead of his son. So Abraham called that place The LORD Will Provide. And to this day it is said, "On the mountain of the LORD it will be provided."[7]

As Abraham and Isaac lifted the exhausted body of the ram to the altar, Beldone opened his eyes one last time. High above The

Beldone moved as far forward as he could and pressed his heaving body sideways against the brush...Socrates slammed headfirst into the small opening his father had created.

Tower, on a single outcropping of rock, stood the silhouette of a young ram. What a fine figure his son was—full of promise, full of the future. And the father took in that final sight with one final thought:

There *is* something worth sacrifice.

The angel of the LORD called to Abraham from heaven a second time and said, "I swear by myself, declares the LORD, that because you have done this and have not withheld your son, your only son, I will surely bless you and make your descendants as numerous as the stars in the sky and as the sand on the seashore. Your descendants will take possession of the cities of their enemies, and through your offspring all nations on earth will be blessed, because you have obeyed me."[8]

• • •

During the entire story of The Tower, Edgar never made a sound. From beginning to end, he stared off into the distance. But Galya knew he was listening intently. Every so often, the raven seemed to cock his head just slightly to hear more clearly.

And now, with the story complete, Edgar remained silent.

The story had touched him deep down inside, where it hurt. Galya wondered if this had been the right story to tell him. He only knew that something was happening inside his friend. And he was too close to lose Edgar now.

Galya decided to tell one final story.

The Healing

In the sixth month, God sent the angel Gabriel to Nazareth, a town in Galilee, to a virgin pledged to be married to a man named Joseph, a descendant of David. The virgin's name was Mary. The angel went to her and said, "Greetings, you who are highly favored! The Lord is with you."

Mary was greatly troubled at his words and wondered what kind of greeting this might be. But the angel said to her, "Do not be afraid, Mary, you have found favor with God. You will be with child and give birth to a son, and you are to give him the name Jesus. He will be great and will be called the Son of the Most High. The Lord God will give him the throne of his father David, and he will reign over the house of Jacob forever; his kingdom will never end."[1]

THE STABLE

The first light of morning hadn't yet broken when Sable's eyes fluttered open. She lay quietly for a moment, adjusting her sight to the darkness around her. She was accustomed to waking before daylight; the pain in her leg often woke her up, and she would have to find a new position and try to drift back to sleep.

Sable could feel the warmth of her mother and the soft rhythm of her breathing; she rolled over and snuggled close. Sable's sleepy eyes moved around the stable and made out all the familiar forms. The two massive shadows at the far end were the easiest to identify; they could be none other than the Bovee sisters, Lyla and Lillie. The rhythmic crunch of the sisters' cud chewing filled the stable. Even in sleep, nothing could stop those two mouths from moving. They spent every waking minute gossiping about the various tenants of the stable. If there was anything to be known about anyone, the Bovee sisters had the information and were quick to pass it on. And if there was nothing to know, they'd happily make something up.

Sable's mother said that was just the way cows were. The sisters and their talk might have been amusing if the things they said weren't so hurtful. For instance, it was the Bovee sisters who started the rumor that bothered Sable the most: the one that claimed her bad leg was God's punishment for some terrible sin in her family. Sable had come into the world with a poorly formed leg, and the sisters were there to see it and suggest the sins behind it. All kinds of evil deeds were discussed. Perhaps, they speculated, little Sable herself was evil.

As Sable grew, she was unable to hop like all the other rabbits did. Her first efforts only served to topple her onto her side. Sable struggled every day, trying in vain to leap gracefully. Finally she found a way to move with a sideways hop—more of a lurch, really.

The Bovee sisters watched without much interest. They never spoke unkindly to her; they never spoke to her at all. The two of them simply stared with rheumy eyes and whispered between themselves. It had been the same on the terrible day when Sable's father had failed to return from his daily excursion—blank stares, knowing nods of the head, and a varied assortment of ideas about God's retribution against these sinful rabbits.

Dawn was just on the verge of breaking on this particular morning, and Rooster was already stirring, getting his powerful pipes ready to announce the new day. Sable enjoyed watching his feathery outline framed against the starry sky. He stretched his wings to their full length, then flapped them noisily several times before folding them back into position. Then he cleared his throat and repeated the process. Sable closed her eyes. Perhaps a few more minutes of rest would be possible. Rooster's routine involved his initial morning regimen of flapping and hacking, followed by an hour of carefully arranging his feathers in preparation for the great barnyard wake-up call.

No animal in the stable carried himself with greater pride than Rooster. None had received such an important commission as that of rousing the world every morning. Who cared about the cows? They carried no authority, and he detested their muttering and snorting and cud munching. The rabbits? Well, they had no real influence. And the sheep? Followers! No leadership in their blood whatsoever.

On the other hand, Rooster saw himself as the handsome, talented, and charismatic leader the world needed. He felt he was the pride of the stable, and all its tenants should look at him worshipfully and count their blessings for having him around.

• • •

"What's an oversized chicken got to be proud of?" Edgar interrupted. "He can flap his wings all day, but he'll never fly. In his dreams, maybe!"

Edgar looked at Galya as though he expected agreement—surely it was an inarguable point. When Galya only stared at him, Edgar continued. "Roosters! Ugh! They strut around as if they own the world, but they're fakes, every one of them. I swooped down on a loudmouthed rooster one day and knocked him clear off his perch. I was sick and tired of his pompous screeching every morning. Maybe I don't *want* to be the early bird every now and then."

Edgar paused and Galya jumped in. "You'll never get the point if you keep commenting on everything, Edgar. Do you think we might get in the rest of the story first?"

He might as well have been talking to a rock. "I'm half blind," continued Edgar, "and if I had only one leg, I could still take out any rooster." The raven seemed for all the world to be carrying on a conversation with himself. Galya stared in disbelief.

"They've got nothing to be proud of," Edgar stated.

"They're insufferable old windbags," he added.

"Nothing but a feeble, clucking chicken in fancy clothes," he further clarified.

"Are you done?" asked Galya.

"I *hate* roosters," Edgar mumbled, to make certain Galya was clear on the point.

"Are you done?" repeated Galya.

"Did I mention they were stupid?" Edgar asked.

Galya realized it was a hopeless situation. When it came to intolerance, the crowd at the stable had nothing on Edgar. Even as his diatribe against worldwide roosterdom continued, Galya resumed the narrative. Perhaps Edgar would find his way back to the story at some point.

• • •

The sun had yet to peek over the edge of the horizon, but Rooster was ready to rip. He cleared his throat one last time and let loose with an earsplitting yell. Sable's eyes flew open, and the sheep scattered in panic—somehow they managed to be surprised by the sound every single morning. Sable rolled to the side just in time to miss being trampled by a ram. Rooster clucked with wicked glee. He knew the ram would never hurt the little crippled hare on purpose. Their kind never did *anything* on purpose; they simply reacted unthinkingly to the moment.

Anyway, as far as Rooster was concerned, it would be no earthshaking tragedy even if Sable *was* trampled. From his perspective, it would simply put the creature out of her misery. Rooster could do without that timid rabbit mother, too. The stable was already overcrowded. Fewer rabbits would mean more food and space for every-one. Rooster crowed one more time, an extended parting blast, then flapped his wings and leaped to a higher perch. It was the best place for his favorite hobby—looking down on all the other animals.

The sun came out and the day grew warmer, but the hearts in the stable remained as cool as ever. Pride, fear, pettiness, and cru-elty abounded among the animals, just as they always had.

The last several days, Lyla and Lillie Bovee had talked unceas-ingly about the latest rumor—the arrival of a new king in Beth-lehem. They claimed the Great Book foretold that he would come to their home. Would this very stable be chosen by a king? The sis-ters chattered about the exciting prospects, expressing their panic over how they might prepare themselves to meet such a dignitary. Surely the king would appreciate all the secrets and inside infor-mation they held on various barnyard individuals. Any ruler worth his salt would make room in his palace for such insightful cattle.

By the end of the day, most of the animals had grown weary of hearing about the king and the old prophecy. Their only comfort was that maybe the big news would divert the attention of the Bovees from gossip about those who lived in the stable; that, at least, would be a relief. But it didn't happen that way. Lyla and Lillie were soon circulating new, unkind rumors about Rooster. The sis-ters saw the stately bird as a rival; they were afraid the king might favor him over them.

With the approach of the arrival time that had been foretold, there was high tension in the stable. Rooster was convinced that if the new king did happen to stop by, he would be embarrassed by the lowly status of the stable. A king would surely see that no roos-ter should have to endure such shoddy society. Every morning, Rooster woke the stable's tenants earlier and earlier. He demanded that the animals begin to follow his noble example, carrying them-selves with all the dignity and pride of noble barnyard life.

This mission became an obsession for Rooster. He railed at the cows to stop chewing with their mouths open and to be silent. He badgered the sheep to demonstrate some courage for a change, and on two occasions he tried to provoke them to fight each other. One night he confronted Sable's mother and insisted that if the king did come, she should keep Sable out of sight. "After all," he argued, "you and Sable are not true domesticated animals anyway. You don't really belong here. And Sable's—ahem—'condition' would be an embarrassment to a true king."

Sable was nearby when these words were spoken. As her mother glared in anger and hurt at Rooster, Sable buried her head deep in the hay and wept. Was that her lot in life—to be an embarrassment? To be kept hidden at the best and most thrilling times?

Maybe Rooster was right. It might be better for her to be trampled by the sheep, or to drift off to sleep some evening and never awaken. She had no father; she didn't fit in with the stable animals, and the wild rabbits had long ago rejected her. There was nowhere to go, nothing to do, and no one to be with but her mother.

When Sable had first heard about the king, her heart had begun beating faster. But now she prayed the rumor wasn't true. The appear-

One night he confronted Sable's mother.

ance of royalty in this stable would serve only to make her feel her unworthiness more than ever. How could a misfit look into the eyes of a king?

••••

Edgar jumped up, agitated. "Didn't I tell you about roosters? If I'd have been there, I would have taken him out! I would have fixed him where he wouldn't have anything to crow about again. He'd have been lucky to outshout a hummingbird when I got through with him—if I'd have been there."

"Well, you *weren't* there," Galya responded.

"How about the sheep? What did they do?" Edgar asked.

"They became very quiet," said Galya.

••••

Sheep don't like making waves—and these were no different. They wanted to be sure that they were in the clear, that they hadn't done anything to get on the wrong side of a king. As the time of the royal visit drew near, the stable became a very sad and dark place to live.

It wasn't dark from lack of sunlight. Even on the brightest day, the shadow of *this* darkness chilled the stable. It came from a subtle kind of evil. Not the kind that causes you to recoil in horror, but an insidious evil that oozes from unseeing eyes, creeps from unkind words, and slithers from uncaring hearts. *That* kind of evil eats away at the soul and destroys all hope.

The Visitor

In those days Caesar Augustus issued a decree that a census should be taken of the entire Roman world. (This was the first census that took place while Quirinius was governor of Syria.) And everyone went to his own town to register.

So Joseph also went up from the town of Nazareth in Galilee to Judea, to Bethlehem the town of David, because he belonged to the house and line of David. He went there to register with Mary, who was pledged to be married to him and was expecting a child. While they were there, the time came for the baby to be born, and she gave birth to her firstborn, a son. She wrapped him in cloths and placed him in a manger, because there was no room for them in the inn.[2]

The night of their coming was so beautiful that Sable couldn't sleep. The evening was cool and moonless, but the stars shone so bright that the trees and the little buildings cast shadows. Sable could see beneath the gate of the stable all the way to the inn. Even the distant hills were softly illuminated. Everyone in the stable was awake and restless.

From his lofty perch, Rooster was the first to see the travel party. He said nothing but shifted his weight from foot to foot and cleared his throat several times. Sable knew something was up, because Rooster was becoming more restless with each passing moment. He was bobbing his head up and down and peering hard into the distance.

Sable was afraid Rooster might think it was dawn and go on to destroy the moment with one of his screeching proclamations. Rooster did break the silence—but quietly. "The king!" he whispered excitedly. "It could be the king!" No one had ever heard Rooster whisper.

Everything grew still. Tension and anticipation filled the air in the stable as all eyes focused on the dignified bird. The silence was broken only by the unintelligible, excited whispers of the Bovee sisters.

Then Sable saw them—a man approaching the inn, leading a donkey. The door to the inn opened and a warm light spilled out, drenched in human laughter and music. The radiant glow revealed a woman riding the donkey; the woman was very heavy with child.

"False alarm," Rooster mumbled with disgust. The door to the inn swung shut briefly, and when it reopened the innkeeper emerged with a lamp. Sable saw the woman climb wearily from the donkey, take the man's arm, and follow the innkeeper to the stable.

Rooster sighed with disgust. "Oh, no—there goes any hope of sleep tonight. How do you like that? Instead of a king, we get a peasant man and a pregnant woman."

The gate whined open, and the innkeeper appeared with the young couple. He was gesturing to an area near the manger, showing them a place to bed down for the night.

The gate whined open, and the innkeeper appeared with the young couple. He was gesturing to an area near the manger, showing them a place to bed down for the night. Then came the part that upset and offended the Bovee sisters: The man led the donkey right into the stable. They eyed each other haughtily. Imagine—a filthy donkey!

None of the stable residents greeted or even acknowledged the new arrivals. Most of them simply looked somewhere else. Rooster completely turned his back and faced the wall at the rear of the stable. The sheep stepped back to provide a little room, but Lyla and Lillie refused to give even an inch. This was a respectable stable. What if it got around that they had shared quarters with a donkey?

Sable relaxed a bit. At least she wouldn't be humiliated in the presence of a king. And yet even the arrival of these quiet people made her nervous. She was barely capable of coping with the treatment she received from the animals; she just wasn't sure she could endure the scorn of people.

The evening should have settled down now, anticlimactic as it was, but it didn't. The innkeeper had barely left when the woman began to cry out. Rooster almost fell off his perch. "Is she going to have that baby right here?" he asked bitterly. "Couldn't she at least hold off until morning?" But much to the consternation of most of the animals, the child was coming.

As the mother struggled to deliver her child, the Bovee sisters rolled their eyes indignantly and huddled together to chew on some new tidbit of barnyard slander. The crying infant finally made his arrival, and the mother tenderly wrapped him in soft fabric and placed him in the manger—*their* manger. It was too much to bear. The stable was filled with the cries of a newborn, the gentle assurances of his parents, and the grumbles of the animals—not to mention the occasional ugly brays of that donkey. The Bovee sisters and Rooster were especially annoyed by the evening's inconvenience, particularly when they had been hoping for something really special—like a royal visit. They had received the very opposite of what they expected.

As the others edged away, only Sable moved forward. The presence of the little family had caused a stirring deep within her heart. She couldn't explain why, but when that child had first appeared, the stable had immediately seemed like a different place. It was certainly brighter because of the unique stars that had commandeered the heavens. But there was something else, too. Sable couldn't quite put her paw on it.

The rest of the animals finally settled down to some serious slumber. Sable didn't sleep in her usual spot that night, but made a little place at one end of the manger where she could see the baby. She was still watching when she fell asleep, and after all the commotion she slept better than she could ever remember.

Sable was awakened by the excited voice of her mother. During the night, the donkey had said something very surprising. He had told the sheep that the king foretold by the Great Book had come after all; he was the very child now lying in their manger. Some scoffed, because, after all, who could believe a donkey?

But Sable believed it all; her heart raced with joy. During the night she had dreamed that this baby was the king, and that he was such a magnificent ruler that he had the power to heal. If the words of the Great Book were true, this king was the Son of God, wasn't He? Wasn't it just possible that He could heal the leg of a rabbit?

As Sable reflected on these things, she noticed that all the animals were awake now and the stable was buzzing with chatter. All of them had dreamed about the baby. It was like fresh air had swept through the stable. No one recognized it at first, but a subtle change had taken place. The brightness Sable had noticed the night before did not come from the sun or the sky; it came from the manger.

At dawn, Rooster had crowed his alarm and then flew down from his perch to inspect the child from close up.

•   •   •

Edgar, who was listening intently, began to squawk. "Fly down? Ha! He didn't fly down! The blustering fowl may have *jumped* down, with his useless wings beating the air, but he didn't fly. Roosters can't fly; they can only pretend."

"Okay, he jumped down, then," sighed Galya in surrender.

"With his useless wings beating the air."

"Just as you say."

"Much better," chuckled Edgar, and he settled back with satisfaction to hear the rest.

•   •   •

Rooster, however he had made it down to the manger, was curious—and that was the curious thing. Rooster wasn't keen on asking questions or making observations. But he was taking much more interest in the child than he had the previous evening, when he had only complained about the infant's howling. Had Rooster, too, dreamed about the child? Rooster harrumphed, cleared his throat, and changed the subject when Sable put the question to him—but he didn't deny it.

Even the Bovee sisters had put aside their lofty airs and were curiously gazing into the stable, watching the child with a sense of awe—and without making any comment. Lyla and Lillie, making no comments? This alone was the greatest miracle yet.

As time passed, the changes continued. The animals closely observed the mother and father caring for their child. And they jostled for position in the stable. "You've had your turn," one would say. "Why not give someone else a chance to stand next to the manger for a while?"

But these protests were mostly mild. There was actually more friendly conversation than ever before in the stable. While there was some disagreement over whether this was indeed the king foretold by the Great Book, things were simply different among the animals. It seemed as though much of the coolness and resentment were melting away in the new radiance, only to be replaced by patience and civility. The presence of one beautiful child had somehow cast out the gossip, cruelty, and resentment that had dominated the stable community.

The next evening, as the animals settled in for the night, Sable did something she had wanted to do since the baby first entered the world. More then anything, she just wanted to touch him. Partly she wanted to see if he was real, and what his human flesh felt like. But more than anything else, she nurtured a tiny glimmer of hope that in touching the child-king, she might somehow be healed. Sable lay on her side and slowly pushed herself forward with her good leg. It was the only way she could move without attracting attention; her awkward form of hopping would have awakened everyone.

Sable kept a careful eye on the parents sleeping nearby. At one point she caught a movement out of the corner of her eye, and she glanced up to see Rooster carefully watching her every move. She knew what came next—he would awaken the entire countryside with some booming, scolding declaration. But this night only a mumble came out as he gently nodded toward the manger and the child. Sable gulped and turned back in that direction.

Finally she was just inches away. Sable was amazed at the sweet smell of the baby's flesh, mingled with the aroma of the soft fabric enfolding him. These were gentle, delicate smells, so pure, so different from the usual barnyard fragrances.

Sable froze. The baby had stirred. As Sable watched, the child turned and seemed to look right into her eyes. Her excitement immediately turned to fear, and she cringed deep into the hay. The unstable hand of the child wavered aimlessly above her. Then, just as she began to plot her retreat, the hand settled gently atop her head and rested there for just a moment.

Sable had half expected some great shock to pulsate through her body. Instead she felt only the softness and warmth of a tiny infant hand. Then, as quickly as it had come, the hand was gone. Sable waited until the child had settled back to sleep, then she moved quickly to push herself back to where her mother was lying. She settled down, closed her eyes, then instantly leaped up again; it was no use trying to contain herself.

Sable woke her mother up and told her everything, in minute detail. Sable's mother had never seen her so animated. "Rooster did not sound an alarm, Mother," she exclaimed. "He allowed me

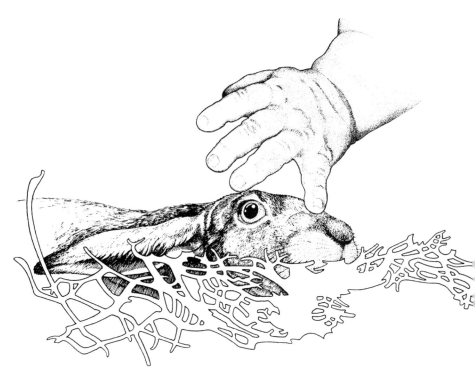

to go! And when I saw the child, the smell was *so* wonderful and I was *so* afraid—until the baby king touched me!" Each time she spoke of the child, she referred to him as "the baby king." "His hand didn't give me a shock or cause me to tremble," she continued. "It just felt so warm and so safe."

About the third time through the story, Sable paused when she got to the part about the baby king touching her. After several seconds, her mother turned to ask her the one question that lingered. It was a question she could barely frame into words. "Can you... Were you..." She continued to stammer, "Did the baby king's touch make you..."

The question evaporated in the air, for Sable's mother saw that her child was lost in a deep, peaceful sleep.

The next morning, by the time the sky began to brighten, the parents and the child were gone. The baby's departure had left the stable darker and emptier than when he was in their presence, yet so much brighter and fuller than before he came. Such a thing seemed impossible, yet it was true.

Sable's mother opened her eyes to see Sable standing at the open stable door, silhouetted against the fresh morning sky. There was something distinctly different about her. When she finally turned toward her mother, her face shone with a light the mother had never seen before. It was as though all the despair and sadness had been washed from Sable's soul. A smile touched her lips as Sable dropped to all fours and made her way back to her mother's side.

The Bovee sisters watched without chewing or commenting. But Sable's mother wept. The first tears were tears of disappointment as she observed her daughter's lame, halting leaps. Then, in the space of an instant, she was weeping tears of pure joy. The sheep moved in to surround the two rabbits as the miracle became clear. Sable was shouting and laughing.

The miracle wasn't the healing of Sable's leg—as everyone had expected. It was something more powerful—the healing of her soul. Sable's mother had never seen her so happy. It's no easy thing for a rabbit to shout, but that's just what Sable did. She was shouting about the child whose infant hand had made her whole for the first time. His touch had opened her eyes to how beautiful and blessed she was—not for what she could be, but for what she was.

With a flurry of flapping, Rooster cleared his throat and crowed his finest aria. On this day it was something less like a raucous alarm and more like a beautiful morning-song. The presence of the baby king had changed the stable forever, and the sounds of praise and celebration went on all day and long into the night. Never was there a more joyful barnyard. Even the Bovee sisters finally were persuaded to join the party, and they had absolutely nothing unkind to say about anyone.

There had been a healing at the stable after all—a healing of the heart!

And there were shepherds living out in the fields nearby, keeping watch over their flocks at night. An angel of the Lord appeared to them, and the glory of the Lord shone around them, and they were terrified. But the angel said to them, "Do not be afraid. I bring you good news of great joy that will be for all the people. Today in the town of David a Savior has been born to you; he is Christ the Lord. This will be a sign to you: You will find a baby wrapped in cloths and lying in a manger."

Suddenly a great company of the heavenly host appeared with the angel, praising God and saying,

"Glory to God in the highest,
and on earth peace to men on whom his favor rests."[3]

•   •   •

"The baby king lives today, Edgar," concluded Galya. "He is the reason life is meaningful. He is the reason I can endure the sacrifice that awaits me. He is the one who heals broken hearts."

Galya braced himself for another tirade about roosters, but Edgar only sat and regarded him quietly. Several times he opened his mouth as if to speak—then snapped it shut again.

"Did you like the story?" Galya finally asked.

Edgar looked away from his friend and hopped to the top rail of the fence. "I have to leave," he muttered thickly, as he leaped into the sky and soared away.

Galya was astounded. He had seen Edgar flippant, irreverent, and even blasphemous. He had seen him laugh so hard he couldn't move, and scream with rage over the smallest offense. But he had never seen him like this. What could it have been in this story that had affected him so strangely? *Perhaps it was all the stories together,* he thought. *Perhaps there was a cumulative effect that had finally taken its toll on Edgar's skeptical spirit.*

One thing Galya had come to realize: He loved this harsh, abrasive old bird.

He longed to see him released from the curse of bitterness that held his heart captive. He also realized there was nothing he could do but wait and hope. Galya walked to the only place in the pen where a few blades of grass survived, and he lay down to wait and to hope. The possibility crossed his mind that he might never see Edgar again.

Edgar wasn't flying in any particular direction, but soon he found himself over the nest that had been his home for so long. He landed on the ground and gazed upward, looking for the familiar shadowy arm that held the nest; then he flew up and landed on the huge branch. He remembered how his mother had sat on the ground, showing him the patterns of light he could always recognize as home and encouraging him to attempt the flight upward.

Edgar remembered her patience as he missed the branch time after time. After a full day of exhausting effort, he was finally able to land on the branch and to find his nest three times in a row. That night, while he rested, his mother brought food. They had celebrated with a feast, then she had thanked God for her beautiful son. It all seemed like a million years ago.

Although he'd never let Galya know it, every Sheep Tale had moved Edgar in a different way. But today's story had engaged him at a deeper level than the rest of them. The details of the human mother and the baby king, the tenderness of the wounded rabbit's mother toward her daughter—and above all, the part about the healing of the wounded heart—all these things had shaken Edgar. He still didn't see the Single Truth to which all the Sheep Tales pointed, as Galya claimed. But at this very moment he was forced to consider something he might never be able to admit.

All his adult life Edgar had believed that his problems would be solved if only he could be healed of his blindness. But today, for the first time, he dared to wonder if it was really his eyes that bore the deepest and truest wounds.

As Galya told the story of the baby king leaving the stable during the night, Edgar became painfully aware that his time with Galya was short. The reality of what was going to happen to his friend hit him with gale-wind force. By the end of the story, he had desperately wanted to make a statement and ask a question, but he could bring himself to do neither.

The statement Edgar wanted to make was really a proclamation of love. He wanted to tell Galya how much he appreciated his friendship, his patience with an angry old bird, and his desire to reach out to him and help him. These things were especially important now, because, for the first time, Edgar believed that help was something he really did need.

The question Edgar wanted to ask was this: Which is more in need of healing—a wounded body, or a broken heart? Is it better to see, or to be free?

As Edgar sat in his nest, a single warm memory washed pleasantly over him. It was the memory of his mother sitting beside him in this very nest, and the gentle tone of her voice saying, "I love you."

He remembered basking securely in the confidence of her love, but never returning the words. He never had the chance—and the next day she was gone forever.

Edgar stood up and shook himself robustly. He would not let that happen again. He would go to Galya, his true friend, and say those three radiant words, even if he had to choke them out. And he would ask his questions, and he would get some answers.

Perhaps if the king still lived, as Galya insisted He did, Edgar would even seek to find Him.

Edgar stepped from the edge of the nest and flew back toward the pen.

10

The Sacrifice

A TIME TO DIE

Galya watched Edgar become a black speck in the sky before vanishing entirely. Then he looked up to see the shepherds approaching the pen. The hands that took hold of him were gentle, and Galya did not struggle with them— only with the many emotions he was feeling.

He felt gratitude because Edgar was not here to see something he wasn't ready to understand.

He felt sadness because he had grown to love the raven.

He felt deep pain because of the burden of misery he knew his friend carried.

He had told the Sheep Tales for Edgar's sake, but Galya himself had been deeply blessed by reviewing them. The old stories had reassured him, more strongly then ever, that these things were happening for a purpose. With the passing of each tale, Edgar's arguments and objections had seemed smaller and weaker. Surely the raven could see that! Surely it was clear by now that he was not searching for the truth but running from it.

As Galya was brought to the master's house, it dawned on him that he felt sorrier for Edgar than he did for himself.

It wasn't that Galya had no fear; it was just that his fear was tempered by hope and truth. Death itself held much less terror for him than the actual *act* of dying. He knew all the gory details of how sacrifices were conducted; from the sheep perspective, they were the stuff of nightmares. But Galya was at peace with all that. The Sheep Tales had given him renewed courage.

That's why he could hold his head high at this moment. His death had meaning and purpose. There was great good that would come from the shedding of his blood. Knowing this knocked the sharp edges off his fear and allowed him to go with a sense of dignity.

He was taken first to the master's house, where he was carefully inspected. Only the best of the flock were considered fit for the altar of God. The master was bound by custom to make sure the shepherd had chosen well. In the presence of his family and all the servants, the master ran his hands through Galya's wool and felt the firmness of his stocky frame. Then he stood back and spoke with satisfaction about the worthiness of this lamb.

The master smiled and nodded his approval to the shepherd. He commanded his family to prepare for the journey to the temple.

In any other circumstance, Galya would have relished the attention and the praise—but this time, high praise only sealed his death. The shepherd tethered Galya to a tree in the courtyard and waited for the master.

• • •

Edgar had half expected Galya to be gone, but he was still stricken by panic. He had returned to find the sheep pen empty.

He rapidly searched every inch of the pen, hoping desperately that his poor eyesight had missed some shadow, some dark corner where Galya might be quietly huddled. But he knew his hope was in vain. Something in his revived heart grasped the awful truth: The time had come; Galya had been taken away.

Yet Edgar searched the pen two times, three times, four times, squawking in pity for his friend and, of course, for his own deep loss.

There was no one around to see him, no one for whom to put on an act, and Edgar let his time-hardened shell fall away. A small trickle of tears came as he hopped around the pen, shouting Galya's name. Soon, however, the dam inside him broke open. Edgar wept deeply, uncontrollably, as he lay in the dust and dirt where his friend had sat so recently, calmly telling his stories.

Not since the death of his mother had Edgar given vent to his deepest emotions in this way. Finally exhausted, he lay still. Then a strange, fearful sound welled up from the deepest part of Edgar's soul. It was a terrible sound—a sound ravens were never created to make. A small hare, feeding just around the corner of the stable, heard the sound, and every strand of fur on his body stood on end. The hare darted away in terror. Any animal of any size would have done the same thing.

It was the sound of distilled, concentrated hatred. Edgar's tearful sorrow was being scorched away by scalding rage.

Throughout the years, Edgar's abrasive manner had alienated him from nearly everyone, even his own kind. A small sampling of his belligerence was usually enough to scare any of them away. And they had all learned to avoid him—all of them except Galya. Edgar had been no easier on the sheep than on anyone else, but Galya had been stubborn about his acceptance—and such an irrational kind of friendliness had only confused Edgar and made him all the more belligerent, simply because he couldn't make sense of such a love. He often flew off in a fit of anger and was gone for days— but he always returned. And when he did, Galya was always there.

Now there would be no one to return to. It wasn't fair.

"It's the same old God!" Edgar snarled. "He took my mother, and now he has taken my friend." His stupid, trusting friend was about to die because of gullible people who believed in a useless God—one who wasn't even powerful enough to save the faithful ones like Galya. Edgar's rage grew until he could no longer remain still. He staggered wildly to his feet, burst into the air, and headed for the temple, still screeching his fury and frustration.

He hadn't been to that human-built place since his mother had died, but he remembered the general direction and a few landmarks.

He hoped he wasn't too late. If there was something he could do to save his friend, he would do it. Either way, he would confront this cruel, weak God face-to-face and tear His eyes out. When the impostor was as blind as himself, maybe the world would see the truth: *There are no gods, there is no God!* There are only fools and those who take advantage of them—predators and their prey.

Edgar zigzagged across the landscape, looking for the first rough blur of a landmark. "The time has come to make things right," he murmured. Little did he realize how accurate that statement would be.

• • •

Galya's master did not take a direct route to the temple. There was one stop he had to make along the way. The master sent his family and servants ahead, down the main road, as he took his sacrificial lamb and headed up the path winding through the hills west of the city. His heart and his steps were heavy, and as he led Galya up the steep trail, he spoke aloud of the things that troubled him. As they walked along, he almost seemed to be speaking to Galya.

Here was a man who had followed Hebrew customs all his life. But he'd experienced something new in recent days—something that had caused him to reexamine everything he believed. A man had entered the city, claiming to be the Messiah. He came riding on a donkey as people cheered wildly. He claimed to be the Son of God, and the master had gone to the city to see what kind of lunatic would make such an outrageous claim.

The man was nothing like the way the rumormongers had described him. Where the master expected arrogance, he found humility; where he expected fraud, he heard sound reasoning; and where he expected politics and manipulation, he found only love.

After encountering this teacher, ritual sacrifice somehow seemed empty—woefully inadequate. He no longer felt the overwhelming sense of cleansing that sacrifice had always brought. The shedding of the lamb's blood had always brought the hope of forgiveness, but now, for some reason, it didn't seem to be enough. As he headed up the hill with his latest lamb, he knew he had come to a turning point. These doubts were surely going to shake the foundations of his faith. If this fine, perfect lamb wasn't enough to offer to God for the people's cleansing—what *could* be presented?

Meanwhile Jesus stood before the governor, and the governor asked him, "Are you the king of the Jews?"

"Yes, it is as you say," Jesus replied.

When he was accused by the chief priests and the elders, he gave no answer. Then Pilate asked him, "Don't you hear the testimony they are bringing against you?" But Jesus made no reply, not even to a single charge—to the great amazement of the governor.

Now it was the governor's custom at the Feast to release a prisoner chosen by the crowd. At that time they had a notorious prisoner, called Barabbas. So when the crowd had gathered, Pilate asked them, "Which one do you want me to release to you: Barabbas, or Jesus who is called Christ?" For he knew it was out of envy that they had handed Jesus over to him.

While Pilate was sitting on the judge's seat, his wife sent him this message: "Don't have anything to do with that innocent man, for I have suffered a great deal today in a dream because of him."

But the chief priests and the elders persuaded the crowd to ask for Barabbas and to have Jesus executed.

"Which of the two do you want me to release to you?" asked the governor.

"Barabbas," they answered.

"What shall I do, then, with Jesus who is called Christ?" Pilate asked.

They all answered, "Crucify him!"

"Why? What crime has he committed?" asked Pilate.

But they shouted all the louder, "Crucify him!"

When Pilate saw that he was getting nowhere, but that instead an uproar was starting, he took water and washed his hands in front of the crowd. "I am innocent of this man's blood," he said. "It is your responsibility!"

All the people answered, "Let his blood be on us and on our children!"

Then he released Barabbas to them. But he had Jesus flogged, and handed him over to be crucified.

Then the governor's soldiers took Jesus into the Praetorium and gathered the whole company of soldiers around him. They stripped him and put a scarlet robe on him, and then twisted together a crown of thorns and set it on his head. They put a staff in his right hand and knelt in front of him and mocked him. "Hail, king of the Jews!" they said. They spit on him, and took the staff and struck him on the head again and again. After they had mocked him, they took off the robe and put his own clothes on him. Then they led him away to crucify him. . . .

When they had crucified him, they divided up his clothes by casting lots. And sitting down, they kept watch over him there. Above his head they placed the written charge against him: THIS IS JESUS, THE KING OF THE JEWS. Two robbers were crucified with him, one on his right and one on his left. Those who passed by hurled insults at him, shaking their heads and saying, "You who are going to destroy the temple and build it in three days, save yourself! Come down from the cross, if you are the Son of God!"[1]

Menacing storm clouds were gathering to the north as Galya's master crested a steep, rocky hill. He paused to watch the tentacles of lightning that snaked across the sinister black sky. He heard the distant rumble of thunder. A monstrous bolt of lightning burst from the heavens and crashed just across the valley, accompanied by a deafening roar of thunder.

The flash of light was so intense that Galya was momentarily blinded. When his eyes finally recovered, he was astonished to see his master kneeling on the ground, weeping. Galya assumed the bolt of lightning had frightened him. But when he followed his master's gaze, he saw the truth. Across the way, low, ominous clouds boiled toward them, blanketing the earth with darkness. But there was a single shaft of sunlight that had broken through the darkness. It revealed a lone figure hanging from a roughly built cross. On that stark scene the master's eyes were fixed.

As the clouds reached the master and his sheep, the air grew deathly still. Even the rumbling thunder faded as the earth seemed to take a deep breath. A voice drifted across the valley and barely cut through the silence.

"Father, forgive them, for they do not know what they are doing."[2]

Then an enormous clap of thunder shattered the sky, and the ray of light around the sad figure slowly faded. Darkness reclaimed the valley, and the sky opened up in a shower of rain. A series of rumbling explosions suddenly broke loose, and the ground shuddered and rolled. Galya stood frozen in fear, staring into the distant darkness. The master now had his face to the ground, and he was sobbing uncontrollably. Galya had never before seen his master weep. He had seemed to be a powerful and confident man, but now he lay in his own tears, oblivious to the rain, dirt, and chaos all around him.

When the earth stopped moving, the master climbed slowly to his feet, his face and clothes dripping with mud. He studied Galya for a moment, then knelt and wrapped his arms around the sheep's wet, woolly neck. Tears were still flowing, but a new look of peace had transformed his face. The master gently slipped the rope off Galya's neck and dropped it to the ground. Then he grabbed the wool on either side of Galya's face and pulled him close.

"It's been taken care of, little lamb," he cried. "You are free."

Then, with a slap on the rump, he sent the bewildered Galya trotting back toward home.

"It's been taken care of, little lamb," he cried. "You are free."

The Final Chapter

Edgar could just make out the boundaries of a small body of water, and he made a slight adjustment in his course. He knew he was headed in the right direction. His anger intensified as he flew on, but so did his heartfelt anguish for his friend. Edgar didn't know it, but the rage that had exploded from his heart had accomplished something all of Galya's efforts had failed to do. It had ripped through the sturdy wall he had so carefully constructed over the years. In order to vent his anger, Edgar had thrown open the sealed door to his heart. The same door that opened to release the venom was still standing open, wide enough for the first time for something else to come in.

The air grew cold and the sky ahead was black. Edgar tried to fly on, but soon the darkness was so overwhelming that Edgar could no longer see well enough to stay aloft. He was about to turn back when he saw a single shaft of light break through the clouds and brighten a small patch of earth below. Edgar banked toward the light and began to descend. As he drew closer, he could hear human voices—but his milky eyes couldn't make out the details. He pulled up sharply and circled from several hundred feet.

Edgar had no fear of people, for he'd never heard of them sacrificing a raven. Still, he had no real desire to land in a crowd at a time when they sounded very angry. But Edgar had no choice. Once the shaft of light disappeared, his landing could be fatal. Even ravens with perfect eyesight can't fly in total darkness. Without a landmark in sight to keep him upright, he would crash and surely die.

A flash of lightning and a crash of thunder moved him to action. At any moment, the clouds might obscure his only hope. He set his wings and spiraled slowly downward, desperately searching for a place to land. At about fifty feet above the ground, he thought he could make out a dead tree.

Cautiously, Edgar began to circle. Normally he would land on the ground and carefully search the branches above for a perch. His poor eyesight made that the safest choice—but not today, with all these

people shouting and hurrying about. He circled lower, keeping the
tree in sight, until finally he set his wings and reached for a foothold.
The whole thing was almost a disaster—Edgar misjudged his speed
and came very close to tumbling into the crowd. It took some quick
work of his wings to keep his foothold, but he made it.

From his perch, Edgar could now make out the forms moving
about below. Their shouting and commotion surged and ebbed. In
the quieter moments, the sound of soft weeping seemed to steal
in from a distance.

Edgar didn't like the situation, but he had no options. He paced
nervously on his perch. Fuzzy as everything appeared, it seemed as
though the forms below were pressing toward him, shouting at him.
At least he was dead certain he was out of their reach; what if he
had lost his balance and fallen among them? Edgar had been around
people a good bit, and he had a pretty fair understanding of their
speech—a few key words at least. But he couldn't understand the
angry shouts of the surging crowd—until one memorable phrase
came floating through.

The phrase was one he recognized from the Sheep Tales: *King
of Israel.*

He loathed the words. This was the One he despised—the One
he was aching so bitterly to kill. In all the chaos, in all his concen-
tration on following his instinct to survive, Edgar had almost forgotten his anger and the reason he had come to this place. Now
his fury was fully rekindled.

These people were shouting "King of Israel," so He *must* be near—
the One responsible for leading his friend away. He wanted so badly
to find that person and to pluck His eyes out! "Give me my sight,"
Edgar squawked to no one in particular. Just then, another recog-
nizable phrase soared over the clamor. The words were *Son of God.*

Edgar began to tremble. This king, this fraud, was claiming to be
the Son of God? A liar of that magnitude had probably already killed
his friend Galya.

Edgar began to pace back and forth on his perch. Never in his
life had he wanted so badly to be able to see. The noise of the crowd

grew louder. Edgar suddenly wondered if they were shouting at him. What if they knew of his plans to attack the king? But they had no way of knowing about Edgar's plot.

It continued to grow darker and darker. Even the shaft of light around Edgar's perch had dimmed until it was only an odd glow set against the gloomy sky. Suddenly a voice cried out, only inches from where Edgar stood.

"My God, my God, why have you forsaken me?"[3]

Edgar staggered and almost fell again. Someone was in the tree with him!

He had been torn by so many feelings these last few hours—outrage and anger, then the need for survival in the frenzy, then hatred toward the one calling himself "the Son of God"—and now a paralyzing fear. The feathers on his neck were standing on end. Edgar had thought he had a safe haven, but a voice had just cried out from this very tree.

He wasn't able to fly in the darkness, and he wasn't safe where he was. Edgar, who tried at all times to be in control, now sat in the dark, completely helpless, as a man's voice screamed out only inches away from him. The raven backed up on his perch as far as possible. As he stood trembling at the very edge, the voice cried out again.

"It is finished." With that, he bowed his head and gave up his spirit. . . .

At that moment the curtain of the temple was torn in two from top to bottom. The earth shook and the rocks split. The tombs broke open and the bodies of many holy people who had died were raised to life. They came out of the tombs, and after Jesus' resurrection they went into the holy city and appeared to many people.

When the centurion and those with him who were guarding Jesus saw the earthquake and all that had happened, they were terrified, and exclaimed, "Surely he was the Son of God!"[4]

That was the very moment when the earth began to shake. Edgar hung on with all his might as the wooden limb beneath him trembled violently. Angry bolts of lightning slashed the sky. There was no place to hide from the thunder, the violent explosions, and the human cries of fear. Edgar thought it might be the end of the world.

Then, from out of the tumult, he distinctly heard and understood six words that paralyzed him with terror. He heard another voice shout above the din, "Surely he was the Son of God!"

As Edgar clung to his foothold, a terrible realization came to him. Edgar knew, for the first time, that the man who shared his tree was the very one he'd been looking for. This was the king—the one responsible for the slaying of Galya, the one he hated, the one he had come all this way to destroy.

And yet, this same man who claimed to be God—was *dead!*

So why did Edgar feel such terror? Should he not feel satisfaction and a sense of fulfilled vengeance? It was impossible, somehow, to sort it out.

Finally the violent storm began to subside, and the earth rested once more. Usually, there was a freshness and a sense of new life in the air after a storm—but not this time. In spite of the rain, there was only a dry, foreboding aura of death. Distant thunder rolled across the horizon as the sky turned reddish gray.

Trembling in the dim, eerie light, Edgar summoned the courage to look around him. He couldn't see any but the closest of objects, nor could he determine what those objects were, given his blindness. Yet, as he edged closer to the center of the trunk, there was no mistaking the blood-caked hand that was held fast to the branch on which he stood. Edgar crept past the hand and peered at the head. It was slumped forward, a crown of some kind encircling it.

Edgar cocked his head, craned his neck, and strained to see the form of a man hanging below him. The body hung completely still; Edgar knew the signs of death well.

It was light enough now for Edgar to leave, but he stayed until the men came to take the body down. The raven had no place to go. He felt he should be celebrating the death of the imposter, yet his heart was as desperate as it had ever been. His friend Galya was

As Edgar clung to his foothold, a terrible realization came to him.
Edgar knew, for the first time, that the man who shared his tree was
the very one he'd been looking for.

surely dead; this powerless king, the focus of his hatred, was dead; his own mother was dead. Edgar was alone.

Warm tears began to flow. They were not tears of anger, or even tears of mourning for Galya; these droplets welled up from the depths of the soul. They were born from the empty desperation that comes when all hope is finally gone. Everything he had cherished had been taken away.

As the body was being removed, Edgar moved to a nearby hill to watch. The men seemed to wrap the body in something before they took it away. Edgar couldn't even feel anger anymore. The words he had heard spoken that day kept playing over and over in his head: *King of Israel. . . Son of God.*

The words of the dying king were bewildering: "My God, my God, why have you forsaken me?" Edgar had carried such a question himself, though he had never been able to put it into words. Had this man, too, felt the bitterness of betrayal? Who had turned against Him?

But the most haunting words of all were the last ones spoken: *It is finished.* Edgar couldn't get the tone of those words out of his mind. He was haunted by the way they were spoken. It wasn't a tone of defeat. The man had not sounded as though He was giving up. Edgar had heard these words from only a few feet away, and he was certain they were delivered with an air of triumph. They had the sound of someone who had just won a race.

The passionate weeping of a woman—surely the man's mother—jarred Edgar from his thoughts. Her cries were unbearable, for he could remember weeping in such a way over the body of his dead mother; here was that same depth of grief, but the mother was crying over her son. Edgar could not remain there another moment.

But where could he go? *It is finished indeed,* he thought. Why suffer through another day straining to see and scrambling for food and scowling at life? It was really all over for him, wasn't it? As this realization sank in, he only half realized he was following the burial party to the grave.

Joseph took the body, wrapped it in a clean linen cloth, and placed it in his own new tomb that he had cut out of the rock. He rolled a big stone in front of the entrance to the tomb and went away. Mary Magdalene and the other Mary were sitting there opposite the tomb.[5]

When the sobbing women finally left, Edgar still sat, high up in a tree overlooking the tomb. He stayed there throughout the night, thinking, of all things, about Galya's Sheep Tales. If only he could speak to his friend one more time; if only there were a way to let Galya know he hadn't missed a single word of those stories. Yes, he'd worn a mask of apathy, but behind the mask he had devoured every nuance of every narrative. Each one had contained a new variation of something Edgar had never known: *hope*—hope for a true purpose in living, hope for a cleansing forgiveness, hope for a new life in another world.

During the telling of the Sheep Tales, Edgar had sensed real hope. But he had been terrified by the prospect of reaching out to take hold of it, because he couldn't bear the possibility of having it snatched away one more time. Even now, after all that had happened, the Sheep Tales once again stirred within him the longing for peace and purpose. If only there were something to cling to.

But there was nothing, nothing at all, because there was evidence fifty feet below Edgar that peace and purpose were nothing but empty dreams. The ultimate hope, the very essence of all Galya's Sheep Tales, lay decomposing in a tomb, and Galya himself had been slain on an altar for no good reason at all. Edgar shook his head. Anger had always been his refuge. It had filled the void, and it had even kept him from acknowledging there *was* a void. But what good was anger now, with the so-called "Son of God" dead?

Edgar hadn't eaten for two days, but he wasn't hungry. He just sat in the tree and waited for something, not really knowing what. He was still there when the guards came.

The next day, the one after Preparation Day, the chief priests and the Pharisees went to Pilate. "Sir," they said, "we remember that while he was still alive that deceiver said, 'After three

But there was nothing, nothing at all, because there was evidence fifty feet below Edgar that peace and purpose were nothing but empty dreams.

days I will rise again.' So give the order for the tomb to be made secure until the third day. Otherwise, his disciples may come and steal the body and tell the people that he has been raised from the dead. This last deception will be worse than the first."

"Take a guard," Pilate answered. "Go, make the tomb as secure as you know how." So they went and made the tomb secure by putting a seal on the stone and posting the guard.[6]

Edgar had dozed for a few moments, and the arrival of the guards startled him. He beat his wings against the air to regain his balance, trying desperately to see what they were doing. Oh, how he wished he could see clearly!

After some angry words and a sharp command, most of the men left. But it was obvious that two or more of them had been left behind to guard the tomb. Occasionally Edgar could hear their whispers and see some movement below.

Edgar went to sleep that night wondering why anyone would find it necessary to guard a grave. It didn't really matter, of course; tomorrow would put an end to all questions. And as he closed his eyes, he realized something new: The king in the grave below had been his last hope. Somehow Edgar sensed this with a deep certainty. They called Him "the Son of God," and He was the one who made all the sacrifices, and life itself, worthwhile. Glubber's experience of forgiveness, Beldone's willingness to sacrifice himself, God's promise to Abraham, the impact of the baby king on the residents of the stable—each of the Sheep Tales offered glimpses of this king who had set out to bring hope to all those, like Edgar, who needed healing.

But the king was dead!

The guards spoke in hushed tones and shifted nervously as the light slowly faded from the sky. Edgar said his farewells to the setting sun. Tomorrow he would leave his perch and fly until he could fly no more. Wherever he fell to the ground would be the place he would die. Edgar had no ideas about what might come after death, but he was convinced it could not be worse than life without hope. *If only the Sheep Tales had been true,* he sighed as he fell asleep.

That night a jumble of dreams paraded through Edgar's fitful sleep. He dreamed of the days when his mother was alive. She was soaring with him over the mountains and valleys, cheerfully describing what she saw below and telling him about the caring Creator who made it all.

He dreamed of Galya. He could see the excited gleam in his friend's eyes as he spoke of Arvid and Glubber and Clarence and of the liberating truths their stories were supposed to have foretold.

He also dreamed of the dying king, whose voice seemed so near. Edgar heard the cry, "It is finished," echoing endlessly in his dreams, each time in a different tone that hinted at some deeper meaning. What was *it*? What was *finished*?

Then he dreamed of the earthquake and the savage bolts of lightning. He shook himself and tried to cast these thoughts away and restore the dreams of his mother, but the lightning would not leave him. It scorched the air with one great, continuous burst of light.

Edgar's eyes flew open. He was wide-awake. The tree in which he sat was swaying violently. The earthquake was real—and so was the great burst of light. The blinding radiance was coming directly from the tomb, and it was painful to Edgar's eyes. He closed them tightly, but the light couldn't be shut out; it broke right through his eyelids.

When Edgar dared to look again, his heart raced with fear and excitement. The whole world had come to life in vibrant, beautiful detail. He saw, above the tomb, a dazzling figure—a great, shining creature in the form of a man, but far more beautiful and powerful. The two guards below drew their swords, took several steps backward, and collapsed to the ground. Edgar could see the emotions on their faces and the colors of their eyes.

Thinking he might still be dreaming, Edgar blinked hard. When he opened his eyes again, he could still see it all—the trees, the tomb, the waving grass, and the morning sunlight—all in perfect, crystal-clear detail. He now understood that the light from the being was so brilliant that it carried the images clear through the obscured vision of his milky eyes.

Just then the light intensified a thousand times as the figure made a sweeping motion
with his hand. Edgar gasped. With
a grinding groan, the huge stone
began to roll away from the
entrance of the tomb. Edgar could
see inside the burial chamber.

There, standing in the doorway
of death, was Life itself!

The man who had been dead—
not *a* king, but *The King*—was alive.
A smile shone from His radiant face as He stepped from the tomb;
it broadened as He seemed to glance, for a flicker of a split second, in Edgar's direction. Then, as quickly as He had come, the risen
King was gone. But the beautiful light remained, and so did the beautiful creature alongside the tomb.

Edgar began to weep once more. It seemed he had been doing
a lot of weeping, but these were unlike any tears he had ever felt
on his face. For the first time in his life, Edgar wept for joy. The light
of the King had made it all the way through his cloudy eyes to the
deepest recesses of his embittered heart.

Edgar had seen the Son of God. Galya had been right all along.
There *was* a reason for living with hope, and dying with hope—just
as Galya had.

After the Sabbath, at dawn on the first day of the week,
Mary Magdalene and the other Mary went to look at the
tomb. . . .

The angel said to the women, "Do not be afraid, for I know
that you are looking for Jesus, who was crucified. He is not
here; he has risen, just as he said. Come and see the place where
he lay. Then go quickly and tell his disciples: 'He has risen from
the dead and is going ahead of you into Galilee. There you will
see him.' Now I have told you."[7]

After the women left, Edgar sat for some time, pondering all that had happened. Slowly it dawned on him that even though the beautiful creature and the brilliant light were gone, he could see! The world was no longer shades of gray; it was filled with dazzling color. Objects were not hazy, featureless forms; they had sharp, defined edges. Edgar watched in amazement as a beetle made its way along the ground, and he suddenly realized he was very hungry. He flew from his perch and landed easily beside his meal.

After eating, Edgar leaped into the air with a screech of joy and soared higher and higher until he was circling far above the tree-tops. In the distance, he saw three crosses silhouetted against the bright blue sky. He flew there and circled above them. It didn't take him long to realize that this was the place where he had seen the King die three days before. He also saw that his perch had not been a dead tree limb, but a crude scaffold of death.

Edgar landed again on that perch. Sadness seeped through him as he saw the dried blood that adorned the crossbeam. But his sadness was quickly swept away, because he knew the man who had hung here just days ago was now alive. This monument to death now stood transformed as a testimony of life!

Edgar took to the sky once again, his heart still surging. There were so many places he wanted to go. He wanted to see the temple and find the place where Galya had been sacrificed. He wanted to see, with new eyes, the places where he and his friend had spent so much time together—the place where Galya had told him the beautiful Sheep Tales. And he wanted to pay a visit to the nest that had been his home for so long. Oh, if only he could tell his mother of the joy that filled him now! How he wished he could thank her for planting the seeds of hope so long ago.

He went there first. After visiting the nest, he flew away, basking in the incredible beauty around him. The nest would never again

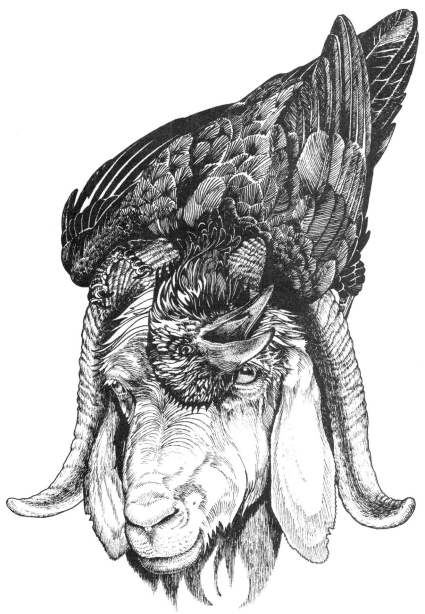

When Galya laughed and nodded, Edgar flew high into the air again and then dove down, landing perfectly between the majestically curled horns on Galya's head. He craned his neck forward, looking right into his friend's eyes.

be his home. He would build a new one, and a new future to go along with it. How wonderful that word sounded as it formed in his brain: *future!* It was a word charged with hope and possibility.

Edgar's heart ached as he saw in the distance the pen where Galya had told him the Sheep Tales. He was amazed at how clear and true those stories now seemed—as clear as his new vision. He arced over the trees just to the south of the pen. Only days before, those branches had been a mass of gray, too thick and obscure to even consider making a landing there. Today Edgar could have chosen the smallest branch within the thickest foliage and landed there with ease.

No sheep were in the pen. It was empty and the gate was open. A large, very white ram grazing at the edge of the forest was the only animal in sight. Edgar swooped down and lit on the same rail where he had last mocked Galya. He was deep in thought as he heard approaching steps. He looked up to see the ram standing several yards away, his head tipped to one side. Then the ram spoke: "Edgar?" he asked tentatively.

Edgar leaped straight into the air, then crashed to the ground. He waddled clumsily toward the ram. "Galya!" he screeched. "Little Lamb! Is that you?"

When Galya laughed and nodded, Edgar flew high into the air again and then dove down, landing perfectly between the majestically curled horns on Galya's head. He craned his neck forward, looking right into his friend's eyes. He was so close that Galya had to cross his eyes to see him clearly. Edgar began to laugh. He laughed so hard it was hopeless for him to try keeping his balance. He lay between Galya's horns, convulsing in laughter as Galya carefully lifted his head to keep from dumping him on the ground.

Finally Edgar caught his breath, regained his footing, and peered once more into Galya's slightly crossed eyes. "I saw the King come out of the grave!" he whispered as he watched a light of hope and excitement flicker in Galya's eyes.

Then, with joy bursting from every feather, Edgar shouted, "I can see, Galya! I can finally see!"

otes

Chapter Two: Paradise Lost

1. Genesis 1:1-3
2. Genesis 1:27-31
3. Genesis 2:8-9, 15-17
4. Genesis 3:1-13

Chapter Three: The Lion's Tale

1. Daniel 6:3-18
2. Daniel 6:19-28

Chapter Four: The Sheepish Prophet

1. Exodus 2:23-3:2
2. Exodus 3:2-4
3. Exodus 3:5-10
4. Exodus 3:11
5. Exodus 3:12-14
6. Exodus 3:15-22
7. Exodus 4:1
8. Exodus 4:2-9
9. Exodus 4:10
10. Exodus 4:13-20

CHAPTER FIVE: CLARENCE

1. Exodus 7:20–21, 24
2. Exodus 9:23–26
3. Exodus 12:29–30
4. Exodus 12:33–39; 13:20–14:9
5. Exodus 14:10–12, 15
6. Exodus 14:21–23
7. Exodus 14:26–31

CHAPTER SIX: A GREAT FISH TALE

1. Jonah 1:1–3
2. Jonah 1:3–17
3. Jonah 2:1–9
4. Jonah 2:10–3:2

CHAPTER SEVEN: AS THE WORM TURNS

1. Jonah 3:3–4:4
2. Jonah 4:5–6
3. Jonah 4:7–11

CHAPTER EIGHT: THE TOWER

1. Genesis 22:1–3
2. Genesis 22:4–5
3. Genesis 22:6–8
4. Genesis 22:9–10
5. Genesis 22:11–12
6. Genesis 22:13
7. Genesis 22:13–14
8. Genesis 22:15–18

CHAPTER NINE: THE HEALING

1. Luke 1:26–33
2. Luke 2:1–7
3. Luke 2:8–14

CHAPTER TEN: THE SACRIFICE

1. Matthew 27:11–31, 35–40
2. Luke 23:34

3. Matthew 27:46
4. John 19:30; Matthew 27:51–54
5. Matthew 27:59–61
6. Matthew 27:62–66
7. Matthew 28:1, 5–7

About the author

Ken Davis is one of the most sought-after speakers in North America. Ken spent fifteen years working for Youth for Christ, and in the last twenty-five years he has traveled the nation as one of its top motivational and inspirational speakers. He has made appearances on television and on stages around the world and is the host of the popular daily radio show "Lighten Up!", heard on over five hundred stations across America. He provides a unique mixture of sidesplitting humor and heartwarming inspiration that never fails to delight and enrich audiences of all ages.

As president of Dynamic Communications, Ken offers seminars and a video series that teach speaking skills to ministry personnel and corporate executives. He has spoken to such groups as IBM, Focus on the Family, The Gaither Praise Gathering, AT&T, U.S. West, Youth Specialties, The Kellogg Corporation, and many more.

Ken was born and raised in the cold north country of Minnesota and is a graduate of Oak Hills Bible Institute in northern Minnesota. Ken and his wife, Diane, now live in Tennessee. They have two daughters. Traci and Taryn are both married and live in Tennessee. The entire family is involved in Ken's ministry, bringing much laughter and liberating truth to people around the world.

Ken is the author of nine books, some of which received national critical acclaim, including winning such prestigious awards as the Campus Life "Book of the Year" award and the Christian Bookseller's Association (CBA) Gold Medallion Award.

Pay us a vist on our Web site at
www.kendavis.com.